Joyriders

Mory rode to the car park in a dream. She was overtaken by the two mountain bikers pedalling fast. They braked, swerved sharply and disappeared round the indoor school, raising dust in her pathway. Mory had the distinct feeling the skids were done on purpose, only this time Dancer didn't flinch. A boy across the yard gave her a thumbs down sign and a frown, his freckles falling into furrows under a shock of red hair. She put a thumb down in reply and shook her head. Lionel had seen the bikers too. Whatever Megan had said had been ignored. They looked like trouble.

Contents

ONE

Bikers

Mory was the last to jump and she felt inexplicably nervous. She was aware of Caroline Spencer's eyes boring into her back, waiting for her to make a mess of it, but that was nothing unusual. Caroline had always shared their riding lessons and although Mory was the person she most delighted in putting down, Josh and Cara didn't escape her horrid comments either. The three other riders watched from the far end of the school as she cantered Dancer to the parallel poles. The approach was just right and Dancer's jump was effortless. Next, throwing a gaunt shadow, was the huge red wall.

"Steady her up a bit," instructed Megan from the side of the arena. Mory sat up, aware that she had only once jumped this high before.

"Steady, girl, steady." Dancer responded, rounding her back under her rider, in time for Mory to urge her forward. Dancer pricked her ears. Three strides to go. One, two, three and they were flying in a giant leap which had them landing on the other side with not a brick out of place. Mory was breathless with relief. Her hand slid down Dancer's neck giving her a stroke of appreciation and delight. No wonder she was nervous, the wall was huge. But in the end Dancer made nothing of it. What a pony!

"Well jumped, Mory," said Megan. "Ride down to the others, please."

Mory gave Dancer another stroke. The pony's response was to fling her head up and veer off in a sudden and unexpected shy which left Mory clinging halfway up her neck.

"Steady, steady," soothed Mory, as Dancer pranced sideways. The cause of the problem was the sudden arrival of two girls on mountain bikes. They came to a stop in a squeal of brakes at the side of the school. Dancer gave them a good long look while Mory hauled herself back into the saddle and straightened the upturned peak of her black and red jockey silk. It was the first time she had worn the silk and keeping it smart was one of her aims.

"Thank you very much," she said. "That was a really stupid thing to do." From underneath their bike helmets the girls looked Mory over. "You frightened my pony!" Mory continued, wanting to emphasize that they had nearly caused an accident.

"Sorry," said one of them, not much meaning it.

"OK if we watch?" said the other, giving a wave. "Hi, Caroline." Mory turned round and saw Caroline lift her jumping whip in salute.

By now Megan was at Dancer's shoulder, concerned for her pupil's safety.

"Well sat, Mory. Are you all right?"

"Yes, thanks."

Megan swung round to the two girls. She looked furious.

"And who might you two be?"

Mory left the bikers to get the telling off she knew they were in for and rode over to the others imagining how perfect her world would be if Caroline Spencer wasn't in it. Caroline sat on Doughnut with the smug, I am better than you for always and for ever look that turned Mory into a ball of fury.

"Don't tell me, Caroline," said Mory. "The bikers just have to be your cousins. Only someone you know could arrive so thoughtlessly."

"Oh, I wouldn't say it was thoughtless," smirked Caroline. Josh slouched forward, stretching up Rustler's neck, to pull his best ghoul face behind Caroline's back. It took Mory a moment to understand what Caroline meant. It left her angered and wondering if the two girls had scared Dancer deliberately.

"The cousins from hell," Josh growled. Cara gave Misty a squeeze and put herself between Caroline and the other two. She could sense Mory and Josh were about to do a brother and sister gang up. Not for the first time did Cara wish it was not Caroline who made up the fourth in their riding lessons.

"Brilliant jump, Mory," she said. "Brilliant."

"Oh, of course, Mory Harper and Midnight Dancer are always brilliant," sneered Caroline. "Goes without saying." Cara shot Mory a warning look. Mory took her cousin's hint and said nothing.

When Megan returned to her pupils Mory wondered what she had said to the bikers. The two were peering sullenly over the rails at the riders.

"Well done all of you. I'll see you tomorrow." That was it, lesson over. Megan put a hand on Dancer's shoulder. "It'll be interesting to see how she goes across country, Mory. She's jumping well and you're seeing the strides better before the jumps now."

Caroline hated it when Megan said anything nice about Mory and Dancer and sent them a keen look of dislike. But after such praise Mory rode to the car park in a dream. She was overtaken by the two mountain bikers pedalling fast. They braked, swerved sharply and disappeared round the indoor school, raising dust in her pathway. Mory had the distinct feeling the skids were done on purpose, only this time Dancer didn't flinch. A boy across the yard gave her a thumbs down sign and a frown, his freckles falling into furrows under a shock of red hair. She put a thumb down in reply and shook her head. Lionel had seen the bikers too. Whatever Megan had said had been ignored. They looked like trouble.

No one said much on the way home from the Penyworlod Equestrian Centre but back at Llangabby

Farm, after the trailer was unloaded and Aunt Olwen had left Mory, Josh and Cara to brush down their ponies, a discussion started.

"You'd think," said Mory, "that after all the trouble we've taken, like looking after her on the sponsored ride, Caroline might be a bit nicer." She brushed vigorously at a line of glued sweat streaking grey along Dancer's black tummy. Dancer flicked back her ears at the vigorous assault. "Nearly done," Mory assured her.

"She just hates Dancer being good," said Josh, not being able to resist giving Mory a surprise dig when she was in such a perfect position for one.

"Hey!"

"Goody, goody Dancer."

"Do that again and you'll regret it."

Josh weighed up the chances of brutal retaliation and decided they were high. He turned back to brush Rustler's chest.

"Caroline's just jealous," said Cara, repeating her favourite explanation for Caroline's unpleasant behaviour.

"Ignore it!" finished Mory and Josh.

"I think you should," said Cara and turned to rub Misty's ears. Misty's eyes half closed with pleasure. "You need a shampoo," Cara cooed. "If the sun's shining when we get home tomorrow you might get one." If Misty understood what was in store for him he gave no sign.

"And what about those two girl bikers?" said Mory. "Hi, Caroline!" she mimicked.

"They're the cousins," said Josh. "The ones she's going to Corfu with."

"If she goes," said Mory. "Hell's bells, I hope she does. No Caroline Spencer for the rest of the holidays. Bliss on a plate!" She threw her arms across Dancer's withers, startling the pony to attention.

"It would be nice," agreed Cara, her cousin's desperation bringing a smile.

"We've had nothing but Caroline Spencer since we came to Wales. I could write a list a metre long of the horrid things she's done."

"No, no, Mory," said Josh. "Not a list. Please not a list." Ignoring him, Mory went on.

"She's always there, sharing our riding lessons, tagging along somewhere, making snide remarks, being foul to Lionel Jones just because he doesn't have loads of money like her. He's the best rider round here only she'll never admit it." Another big sigh, arms flung back across Dancer's withers. Expecting it this time, the pony flicked her tail in protest.

"I know what you mean," said Cara.

Aunt Olwen bustled into the yard.

"Goodness gracious," she said. "Haven't you turned them out yet? Hurry up."

"Can they go out up here?" asked Cara. "Dad said they were to go down to the Black Rock paddock but up here would be easier for the morning."

"One more night up here will be fine," said Aunt Olwen. "Glyn must have forgotten about the cross country lesson. They can go down to Black Rock after. And don't forget, Cara, you're helping me with the egg round." Aunt Olwen made to go in but turned back with a parting shot. "And something needs to be done about that tack. A sponge down at the very least." They looked at one another and groaned.

"Might as well get it over with," said Mory, undoing Dancer's lead rope. "Get it done before lunch. I said I'd help Dad this afternoon."

"More pocket money?" enquired Cara.

"Of course," replied Mory. "And I've got something

for you. It got buried under a pile of clothes which is why I forgot."

"Oh, yes!" said Josh.

"What?"

"Don't say," warned Mory. "It's a surprise. Come down after the egg round and I'll give it to you." And Mory led Dancer towards the pony paddock.

When all the chores were finished Mory and Josh set off down the rutted track to their home at Black Rock. A squeak of bike brakes behind them caused them to jump to the side. A gleaming new mountain bike bumped to a halt and a face grinned at them from underneath a shiny black and white bike helmet spiked with wisps of blond hair.

"Felix," gasped Mory. "Where did you get that bike from? It's brand new."

"Cool or what?" said the boy, pulling off his helmet and scratching his head. Josh ran a finger admiringly along the handlebars. The words Star Rider III were painted in yellow and green letters on the black frame.

"Cool," said Josh. "Can I have a go?"

"Certainly not," said Felix. "It's too new to take a chance on a squirt like you riding it. It's mine." Felix pulled on his helmet. "Hands off." And he set off down the track leaving the dust to rise behind him.

"Never mind, Josh," said Mory, giving him a friendly shove. "You've got Rustler. He's much better than a bike any day."

"Looks like Felix's gone odd on us again," Josh said. "I fancied a go too."

"He'll change his mind when it's not so new. Bet you."

Turning into the Black Rock yard they were met by two bottom-wriggling puppy bundles who tried to climb Josh and Mory's jeans, they were so excited to see them.

"Hello, pups," said Mory. "Down Nip. Down Pep. Hell's bells, Josh, they're on springs." Josh lay obligingly on his back and the puppies climbed over him, Nip licking him all over the face. Mory recognized Nip, Josh's own special puppy, by the white tip to her black tail. Uncle Glyn's puppy, Pep, had a completely black tail.

"Yuk, Josh. How could you let her?" said Mory, screwing up her face. Josh pushed the puppy off and rolled over.

"She likes to say hello," he grinned, wiping his mouth with his sleeve.

Across the yard, leaning against the pottery wall, was Felix's gleaming bike.

"Look," said Mory. "Felix didn't go far." Josh raised an eyebrow enquiringly.

"Might get a go after all," he said, picking up Nip and swinging her front paws over his shoulder while Pep jumped up trying to bite Nip's tail.

"Let's go in. It must be lunch-time," said Mory, whose tummy was beginning to groan. She poked her head round the pottery door.

"Hi Dad, is lunch ready? I'm starving."

"You'll have to ask your mum. She's lunch provider today. Tell her there's an extra one. I expect Felix would like something to eat, eh Felix?" Felix nodded. He was watching David wedge a piece of clay, kneading it as if making bread. It was obvious he was longing to try it himself.

"Felix is in with Dad," Mory informed Josh, who had gathered both puppies into his arms and was collapsing under the strain. He let them slide to the ground.

"He's dead keen on pottery," said Josh.

"For how long? Riding lasted about two seconds until he realized it was more difficult than he thought," said Mory, remembering all the fuss Felix made about wanting to learn and how quickly he lost interest. "Now it looks like it's mountain biking." Eyeing the splendid machine against the wall Mory wondered how long the biking would last.

"What's for lunch?" asked Mory, tripping over a wellington boot and falling through the kitchen door.

"Cold soup, bread, cheese and salad," replied her mother. "Nice and healthy."

"It must be. The soup's green," said Mory, startled by its vibrant colour.

"Cucumber and watercress. An experiment for when the Spencers come to supper."

"The Spencers! Why do you have to have them?"

"A thank you for all the hard work they put into making the barbecue a success after the sponsored ride. I noticed you enjoyed it. Also Megan and Ian are coming. I've managed to pry them away from their horses for a few hours. And Glyn and Olwen will be here too, and maybe Mrs Ashfield. It's almost a party."

"When?" asked Mory, chilling inside until she felt as cold as the green soup. The Spencers might bring Caroline. That would be too much.

"Next Sunday. And could you tidy up those boots," asked Sheila. "Someone is going to break their neck on them in a minute and I don't want it to be me."

Mory shuffled to the porch with a frown of the deepest misery and piled the boots in a corner.

"What do you want to have a party for?" she asked,

coming back into the kitchen and slumping on to a chair, elbows on the table, chin in her hands. "I mean, what for?"

"I've just told you why. Caroline won't be coming, if that's what's worrying you. She'll be staying at home with her cousins."

"Hi Mum," said Josh. "Felix wants lunch. What are we eating?"

"Green soup," groaned Mory. "And it's cold." Josh looked in the saucepan.

"Slime," he said.

"Josh, please," said Sheila. "Mory, set another place at the table. And stop looking as if the end of the world is nigh."

The green soup was a success with the adults. Felix refused it point blank and Mory and Josh tried it and pulled faces.

"All the more for those that like it," said David, reaching for Mory's bowl.

"Before I forget, Felix. Could you take this invitation to your grandmother?" Sheila asked, getting up to fetch an envelope from the mantelpiece with Mrs Ashfield's name on it. "She's the only person I can't reach by phone." Felix stood up and shoved the envelope in his pocket.

"Better warn her it's green soup," said Mory, under her breath, before stuffing the corner of the cheese sandwich she'd made into her mouth.

After lunch, standing in the cowshed surrounded

by a pile of newspapers and boxes and a list of which pots were to go where, Mory contemplated an afternoon of wrapping. Her head felt stuffed into a black cloud. It was the sort of mood that meant she was having a bad dose of *I hate Caroline Spencer and anyone else who has anything to do with her* which at this moment included her mum and dad. Fed up, she scrunched a piece of newspaper and threw it across the cowshed. Instantly, there was a streak of fur as Splodge, Mory's cat, pounced. All four paws landed on the paper and, with back arched, he lifted himself from the ground, tossing the paper away before darting off to hide behind a cow stall. Mory screwed up another piece and bowled it temptingly close. Splodge pounced again and, lying on his back, shredded the paper with his sharp claws.

"Daft cat!" Mory picked him up. Splodge loved cuddles and immediately began to purr, pounding his front feet against Mory's chest, causing little needle pinpricks. Used to it, Mory wrapped the offending paws in the palm of her hand.

"I don't know, Splodge, it's awfully nice living here, much better than Waring, isn't it? I mean, we've got Cara and Uncle Glyn and Aunt Olwen up the hill at Llangabby. A farm of our own to live in. I've got Midnight Dancer and you, Josh has got Rustler and Nip, and Cara's got Misty. The only friend I miss is Hannah and she's fed up with being stuck in Waring. She can't wait to meet everyone. And Lionel Jones, the best rider at the Penyworlod Equestrian Centre, is our friend too and Felix Ashfield, unless he goes off us again. We've got Megan and Ian Reece to help us be better and better riders. But all that is ruined because for ever and always there is Caroline Spencer ready to spoil things. Like today in the riding lesson. Dancer was brilliant but Caroline would never admit it, even though Megan said how good she was. And it matters, it really matters that Caroline is so horrid. What am I going to do, Splodge?" Splodge replied by purring louder. "Daft cat!" Mory nuzzled her nose in his fur. "You're no help. No help at all."

David popped his head around the cowshed door.

"How are you getting on, Mory?"

"Just starting." She put Splodge down.

"Now you are clear on which pots are to go in which boxes?"

Mory waved the instructions. "Couldn't be more clear," she said. "Trust me, Dad. I'll get it right."

"I'll trust you though thousands wouldn't," he quipped. Mory looked out of the grimy window.

"Did Felix let Josh have a go on his bike?"

"No. Resolutely refused. Josh has taken the puppies up to Llangabby to be with Mab."

"Has Felix gone home then?"

"He's in the pottery wedging clay."

"Well, where's his bike? It was against the wall but it's gone."

TWO

Stolen

Felix stood in the yard shouting. He was white with rage and his yelling got louder and louder.

"I'll kill them. I'll kill them. Whoever's got it, I'll kill them."

"Steady, old chap," said David, putting a hand on Felix's shoulder. Felix swung away.

"Don't touch me," he snarled. "It should have been safe. It was leaning against your pottery wall. You said it was safe." David was taken aback but before he could say or do anything Felix turned and ran.

"He's always like this when he gets upset," said Mory. "You have to wait for him to calm down."

"I see," said David. "Good at explosions, is he?"

"He has just lost his brand new mountain bike. Are you sure Josh didn't borrow it for a go?"

"Quite sure," said David.

"Well someone's taken it. There must be a thief."

"Dash it!" said David. "We've been here all the time." Mory said nothing but, from her own experience, knew how easy it was to sneak across the yard without being seen. It would have been simple to take the bike without detection, she knew that for a fact. The puzzling thing was, who had? Black Rock being so remote, it was unusual for people to come this way unless to visit.

"Well," she shrugged. "Better go and look for it. See if there are any clues or anything."

"I suppose so," said David. "A quick search to make sure it's really gone and then I'll drive over to Hill Farm and tell Mrs Ashfield what's happened. It wouldn't be fair to blame Felix. What bad luck!"

David called Sheila and the three of them scoured the yard, the stables, the tack room and the barn. No bike and not a hint of what might have happened to it.

"So someone must have stolen it?" questioned Sheila. David shrugged.

"Looks like it. I'll tell Mrs Ashfield and see if I can find Felix on the way."

"I'll keep an eye on things here," said Sheila. David nodded.

"Coming, Mory?"

Bumping up the track in the car Mory wondered if there was a burglar on the loose or if there was a more obvious explanation. If there was she couldn't think what it might be.

"Felix has got quite a temper," said David. "Have you seen him like that before?"

"Oh, yes. He can scream and kick and tell lies too."

"Really?"

"But we saw the bike so we know that's true," said Mory. "He gets over it after a bit."

"I'm glad to hear it," said David.

Mory remembered what Mrs Ashfield had said to her about Felix needing friends of his own age to help him get over the horrid time he'd had at school. Mory wondered how the school had managed to be so hateful until she thought of a school with every pupil like Caroline Spencer. She was instantly sorry for Felix if it was anything like that.

David turned the car into the yard at Llangabby. There was no Land Rover which Mory guessed meant Aunt Olwen and Cara were out delivering eggs. Uncle Glyn had a wheel off the tractor and Josh was playing with Mab and the puppies.

"Josh, have you seen Felix?" David asked, getting out of the car. "His bike's disappeared and he's rather upset about it."

"No, I haven't." By the look of surprise on Josh's face it was clear that he'd had nothing to do with it.

"What happened then, David?" asked Uncle Glyn, wiping a handkerchief across his weather-beaten face and round his hot neck. "Has it been stolen?"

David shrugged. "Must have been someone on foot. We'd have heard a car."

"Shame Nip's not a bit older. She'd have seen them off for you." Mory smiled at the thought, knowing how pleased Josh would be when Nip was grown up enough to do just that. "Going to report it?" Uncle Glyn asked. David sighed.

"I'll let Mrs Ashfield know first. Coming, Mory?"

"Do you want to come, Josh?" Mory asked before getting back in the car.

"Mab and I'll go and look for it," he said. "If you don't mind me borrowing her, Uncle Glyn?" Uncle Glyn let his eyes rest on his black and white border collie before shoving his handkerchief back in his pocket.

"Fine by me," he said.

"It's probably miles away by now," said Mory.

"You never know," said Josh and gave a whistle which brought Mab running.

"Get in the car, Mory," said David.

He turned the car round and they drove over the cattle grid and along the hilltop track that led to Mrs Ashfield's cottage, Hill Farm. The car bounced and bumped across the ruts. Mory clung on while the car squeaked and groaned in protest.

"Sorry. A bit fast," said David, slowing down. "Be better when I get a Land Rover."

"A Land Rover?" asked Mory surprised.

"We may well need a four wheel drive vehicle in the winter."

"A Land Rover!" Mory's thoughts became side-tracked by vast snow drifts until a more immediate use occurred to her. "You'll be able to tow the horse trailer and take us to shows and everything when Aunt

Olwen's too busy."

"Perhaps," smiled David. "The main reason for getting one is to fetch supplies and get you to Aberdawl for school."

"I won't mind not going to school in the snow. I could help Uncle Glyn on the farm or you in the pottery instead." David smiled.

"That's very nice of you but you're forgetting that your mum has to make every effort to get to work, being a teacher, and if she goes you kids go too."

Mory was beginning to think there might be a disadvantage in having your mum a teacher in the school where you were going to be a pupil. But she didn't think about it for long. David drove between the rock crop and the land fell into a dip. Way past Hill Farm, on a distant ridge, Mory spotted three figures bike riding along one of the sheep tracks.

"Look Dad, over there?"

"Where?" asked David, only looking up for a second he was so busy avoiding ruts.

"Up on the skyline, right in the distance, three people on bikes."

"You've got good eyes," he said, slowing. "I can't see them."

"There!" said Mory, pointing. "They've gone. I think they're going down towards the fallen oak. They'll have to come back up this way to get back to the lane and on to the road."

"I'm sure they won't have anything to do with the

disappearance of Felix's bike," said David. "Whoever took that is long gone."

"I suppose," said Mory.

They bumped to a halt alongside Mrs Ashfield's battered green Range Rover while Mory's curiosity grew. It was rare that anyone came on to the hill this way. She wanted to know who the bike riders were or at least to get a closer look. As they climbed from the car, Hector's deep bark began inside the house, bringing Mrs Ashfield to the door to see who her visitors were. Hector bounded to the gate and was so magnificent that Mory thought that if she ever had a dog she'd have a deerhound like him. She stroked his shaggy face and he replied by planting several wet

licks on the back of her hand.

"What a nice surprise," said Mrs Ashfield. "Come in."

David pushed the gate open and Hector stepped politely back. Mory was thrilled to have been invited indoors. It was a chance to see what Mrs Ashfield was painting. When she grew up Mory wanted to be a famous rider first and second an artist like Mrs Ashfield. Ever since Mrs Ashfield had come to live at Hill Farm she'd taken every opportunity to look at her pictures. She followed David into the house.

"Is Felix not back?" David asked.

"Not yet," said Mrs Ashfield. "I thought he would be following you. He has been with you, hasn't he?"

David explained about the stolen bike and Mory studied the room. She breathed in the sharp smell of oil paint. On Mrs Ashfield's easel stood a half-finished painting of a fox crossing the heather on a clear summer's morning. Mory could almost feel the freshness of the air. Sitting on a small table beside the easel was a proper artist's palate daubed with green, yellow, red, blue and white paint. Tubes and tubes of different colours lay on the table, two with their tops off. A large glass jamjar held a selection of brushes sitting in a murky liquid and several paint covered rags were strewn about. On the floor sat a large bottle marked "Turps".

Wow, thought Mory. Just like a real artist's studio. She had no time for further looking. Mrs Ashfield called Hector and she found herself bustled out of the front door.

"Hector and I will look for him," said Mrs Ashfield.

"We'll all look," said David. "I assumed he would come home. But it seems like he's gone looking for the bike by himself."

"I'll walk back," Mory said. "Then we can all search in different directions."

"What a disappointment for him," sighed Mrs Ashfield. "The mountain bike was a late birthday present from his parents. If it really has been stolen I'll never hear the end of it."

Mory had a good idea of how Felix must be feeling. Once, when she thought she'd lost Midnight Dancer, it seemed like the end of the world. She set off on the track to the fallen oak just in case the bike riders were still there. She came down into the dip where the stricken tree lay, moving from rock to rock to keep under cover. Then she heard them, girls' voices, giggling, excited, elated. She slithered snake-like towards the fallen trunk, keeping low in the heather. She paused, close enough now to make out what they were saying.

"It was brilliant. That'll show her." The hairs on the back of Mory's neck prickled.

"I bet she's looking all over the place for it." The voice was unmistakable. It belonged to Caroline Spencer. Mory raised her head above the heather.

Three mountain bikes leaned against the oak. One of them was Star Rider III.

"Zap her off her high horse," said a voice Mory didn't know. "I bet she's bananas wondering where her bike is."

"I hope so Trish," said Caroline. "I hope so." It was them, thought Mory. They think they've stolen *my* bike.

"Next time we'll turn her horse loose," said the third girl.

"No," said Caroline. "The others might get out too."

"So what?"

"Well, something serious might happen to them."

"Chickening out?"

"No, Phoebe, it's not that," said Caroline. "If Mummy and Daddy find out about us hiding the bike, we'll be in for it. But if we let out ponies they'd go mad."

"Caroline's a scaredy cat, scaredy cat," chanted the

one called Phoebe. Mory wriggled closer and peeped over the fallen tree. All three had their backs to her.

"Yes, and what about if they let Doughnut loose getting their own back or something? What about that?"

"We'd keep guard night and day," said Phoebe.

"And what about when we're in Corfu? Mummy said that Cara's parents would look after Doughnut for me. Imagine. She'll be with the enemy."

"Pack it in, Phoebe," said Trish. "Caroline's right. We can't let out ponies." The cousins got up and drifted down the hill.

"Why is there a path worn round this tree?" asked Phoebe. "It goes in a figure of eight."

"Mory and that lot use the tree for a jump," said Caroline.

"They jump that tree?" Both cousins turned round to look. Mory ducked. The cousins were as alike as two peas. Mory savoured the surprise – twins!

"On their ponies, stupid," said Caroline.

"I guessed that. I'm not a horse freak, that's all." There was a silence and for a moment Mory thought they had seen her.

"I know," Phoebe cried. "We can let the air out of her tyres before she gets the bike back. Why didn't I think of that before?"

No chance, thought Mory and sprang. She grabbed Star Rider III, swung it round and raced up the path. From behind came a shout of rage.

"Bring it back!" They must be joking. She'd got Felix's bike and no way were they getting it back. She glanced over her shoulder. They were following her, shouting for her to stop. Mory wanted to shout – Long walk home, Caroline! – but restrained herself. She needed all her energy to push the bike.

At the top of the path Mory jumped on a pedal and

swung her leg over. Feet straining and hands pulling, she heaved herself up the track to the rock crop. She couldn't wait to tell Felix what she'd done. The twins raced after her up the hill and looked like big trouble. But she'd beat them back to the Llangabby yard – she was sure of it. At the cattle grid she swung off the bike and wrenched the gate open. Hauling the bike through, she closed it behind her.

"Made it," she puffed.

In the distance the twins were still yelling. Mory grinned. They probably hadn't recognized her from yesterday. They'd only seen her with her crash cap on, underneath her black and red silk. They sounded wild. If they thought a stranger had stolen the bike they would think they were in real trouble. Well they can stew, she thought, Caroline can tell them when she catches them up. They deserve a fright.

Mory swung herself into the saddle and pedalled for the Llangabby yard. She was there before the twins realized where she had gone. She leapt from the bike and hid behind the wall. She had the satisfaction of hearing them whizz past and of watching them disappear down the lane and round the bend on a fruitless chase. Mory hurried the bike into the barn and, for absolute safety, hid it in the horse trailer. She wanted to get clear of the yard before Caroline came running.

THREE

Red Faces

Racing from the barn, Mory was greeted by Hector and Mab, tails wagging, noses nuzzling.

"Hello dogs," she said. "Everyone indoors?" Mory burst into the Llangabby kitchen, desperate to tell what she had done. There was quite a gathering. Aunt Olwen bustled with tea things, Uncle Glyn was in his chair, Mrs Ashfield, David and Felix were at the table while Josh and Cara put out biscuits.

"Guess what?" Mory said to the sea of astonished faces. "I've found Star Rider III." She waited for the expected gasp of happy surprise. It didn't happen.

"You can't have, Mory," said Josh, breaking the silence. "We found it."

"But I have. I've just put it in the horse trailer for safety."

"No," said Josh. "Someone hid it in the bottom paddock behind the brambles. Mab sniffed it out."

An uncomfortable thought occurred.

"Mory, what have you done?" asked David. The thought burst like a water-filled balloon – Caroline and Felix have the same make of bike.

"Oh, pig's swill!" spat Mory, furious with herself.

"What's happened?" asked David, getting up.

"Nothing," said Mory. "Forget I ever spoke." And she stomped back outside to find Caroline walking purposefully across the yard.

"Where is it?" Caroline's tones were strident.

"Tit for tat," said Mory, standing her ground. The twins swung into the yard, adding reinforcements. Those in the kitchen spilled into the yard too and David, Josh, Cara and Felix gathered round, curious.

"Hello, Caroline," David said. "You look hot."

"I've been running," said Caroline, pointedly. "I want my bike back."

"OK, OK, I'm fetching it," said Mory. Caroline was the colour of a boiled beetroot. She took a deep breath. Mory jumped in quickly before she said anything. "The thing is it's exactly the same make of bike as Felix's and his went missing." She didn't take her eyes from Caroline. "I thought yours was his. Hardly surprising really considering the circumstances. It was an easy mistake to make." Then she turned leaving Caroline open-mouthed and went to the barn to fetch the bike. Josh dashed after her, grinning at the error. He helped get it out of the trailer.

"Honestly," whispered Mory. "How was I supposed to know she'd got a Star Rider III? But it *was* them. They nicked Felix's Star Rider. I heard them talking about it."

"Does that count as a double whammy?" giggled Josh.

"Oh, shut up," said Mory, wondering what she'd started. "I'm telling you those twins are much worse than Caroline. We're really going to have to watch it with them around." She wheeled the bike outside and handed it over.

"Thank you so much," said Caroline, as if she had been handed the crown jewels.

"Would you girls like some refreshments?" said David. "There's juice and cola in the kitchen." Mory flushed bright red and all but kicked her father.

"No thank you, Mr Harper, I think we should be getting home now. My parents will wonder where we've got to. We're quite late enough as it is." Caroline shot Mory one of her dagger looks and pushed her bike out of the yard. With sullen stares the twins followed.

"Oh dear, Mory," said David.

Mory shrugged.

"I thought they nicked it so I nicked it back. It was them, you know. Who hid Felix's bike."

"Was it?" said Felix and made to go after them. David quickly put out a restraining hand.

"Let sleeping dogs lie, Felix." Sleeping dogs, thought Mory. There are no sleeping dogs round here. And as if to prove a point Nip and Pep bounded across the yard, delighted to have discovered human beings.

* * *

Felix sat on Mory's bed kicking against the bed leg. Then he sprang up and crossed to the window.

"It's quite safe now, Felix," said Mory.

"Just making sure," he mumbled.

Star Rider III was in the cowshed padlocked securely to an iron ring in one of the cow stalls.

"No one can nick it unless they've arms as strong as a robot," said Josh.

"If Cara doesn't come soon," grumbled Mory, pulling back the flaps of a cardboard box sitting in the middle of the floor, "it'll be too late. What is she doing?"

The sound of running feet coming down the track caused Mory to lean out of the window.

"Where've you been?"

"Cleaning my tack," panted Cara. "Let me in the front. It'll be quicker." Mory leapt from the window and dashed downstairs. Felix looked outside one more time.

"What would you have done if your bike had been stolen?" Josh asked. Felix shrugged.

"I'm not thinking about it."

"I'd track down the thief and set an ambush," said Josh.

"I'd like to set an ambush for those girls," growled Felix. "I'd dig a pit so big that they'd fall in. Then I'd shoot spears down on them. That'd show them." He lunged an imaginary spear at the door just as Mory and Cara burst through it.

"Close your eyes and hold out your hands," ordered Mory.

"Must I?" said Cara.

"Yes, you must." Cara did as she was told while Mory rummaged amongst the packing paper in the box. She pulled out a pair of brown saddlebags which she laid across Cara's arms.

"Open your eyes."

"The saddlebags! Brilliant! We can fit loads of stuff in these. Did they send the right number?"

"Four as requested," said Mory. She had sent away for them from a mail order catalogue. They had each paid for their own out of their savings and Mory had paid for an extra pair for Lionel from her "helping David in the pottery" wages. She knew that Lionel's dad never gave him any pocket money and that any money he earned had to do for all sorts of things. "I'll give Lionel his tomorrow." Each pannier had a flap fastened with a strap and buckle. Cara undid the straps and examined the insides. There was plenty of room and there were special eyelets for tying the bags to the saddle so they wouldn't slip off.

"They're great. A million times better than a ruck-sack bouncing on our backs," she said. "I think we should go on a picnic ride to celebrate."

"Lionel and Ning too!" cried Mory.

"Of course," grinned Cara. "We must try them out."

Josh looked thoughtful.

"We've got to find a new den. That's what we need to do."

"I'll help." Felix was on his feet ready to go. "Can I?"

"If you can keep up," said Mory.

"On my bike I can."

"Only if you're nice to Lionel," said Cara resolutely. There was a moment of thoughtful silence.

"I'll be nice to him if he'll be nice to me," said Felix at last. "Tell him that." He rubbed his nose. "I'm going home now."

Josh followed him out.

"Can I have a ride round the yard before you go?" The girls exchanged a look and smiled.

"Josh'll wear him down in the end," said Mory.

"The good news," said Cara, pulling a tatty piece of paper from her pocket, "is that Mum says she'll take us to the Llantrist pony show the Saturday after next. Which means we can fill in our entry forms."

"Great," said Mory, reaching over to unpin hers from her notice board. "And guess what! Dad told me he's getting a Land Rover. That means he or Mum can take us to shows whenever Aunt Olwen is too busy."

"Wowee," said Cara.

"It's for the snow," Mory went on. "I never thought we could be trapped by snow drifts down here. Tracker dogs might have to sniff us out and food parcels be dropped by helicopter."

Cara looked at her cousin as if she was taking leave of her senses.

"It's not the Arctic, you know. You wouldn't need sniffing out. We know where you are. Dad would snowplough you out with the tractor." Cara laughed. "Honestly, you're not a flock of sheep!"

Cara plonked her entry form on Mory's table and reached for a pen.

"Let's get on with this. What are you going to enter?"

When it was nearly bedtime, Mory walked up the track with Cara to Llangabby to say good night to the ponies. The entry form for the Llantrist show had been easy. She'd put down Best Turned Out Pony although she didn't think she stood much chance of winning that, the Handy Pony class to see if Dancer had improved on her last attempt, and the Novice Showjumping class. She hoped Dancer would jump as well as last time. Fingers crossed and keep practising, she told herself.

"I wonder when Caroline Spencer's going to Corfu," she said.

"No idea," replied Cara. "I don't think she knows yet."

"If her parents are coming to supper next Sunday it won't be until after that."

"At least Caroline's not coming," said Mory. "After pinching her bike I would have died."

"They started it," said Cara as they turned into the Llangabby yard.

"I suppose," said Mory. She felt her cheeks turn pink with the embarrassment of it. "I never thought she'd have a bike the same."

"Another of your rash decisions."

"Don't, Cara."

They strolled across to the paddock and Mory

patted the bulging supply of pony nuts in her pocket. Standing in a huddle, flickering their tails in lazy disharmony, the three ponies gently dozed. Mory climbed the gate.

"Coming to say good night?" she asked.

"Might as well." At their approach the ponies flicked their ears forward, interested in a sleepy sort of way. As soon as Mory's hand went in her pocket they ambled over. Pony nuts were always well received.

"Here you are then," said Mory, giving each a handful and pushing Rustler's nose out of the way when he shoved for more. "Greedy boy," she said, listening to the contented crunching which she loved. She ran a hand down Dancer's sleek neck. "Night,

night lovely pony." One arm lifted over, the other under, she hugged the black pony's neck. Then, pulling a few stray wisps of mane to lie with the rest, she followed Cara back to the gate. Dancer gazed after her and only turned back to the others when Mory had climbed the gate and could be seen no more.

The following morning was hustle and bustle. The ponies were groomed, rugged and booted in record time. They decided to tack up when they got to Penyworlod. The ponies were loaded in the trailer and hay nets were tied to the back of the ramp. They were ready. Mory was bursting with excitement. She was longing to jump real cross country fences. The nearest to it was the fallen oak and she had done that so many times it seemed boring. Boring! She could hardly believe she could think such a thing when only a few weeks ago it had seemed the most frightening thing in her whole life.

"Come on, Mory," called Aunt Olwen. "You're in a dream this morning. Got your hat?"

"Yes, no!" Mory went running for it.

"It's just that it's the cross country," she said when at last she clambered into the Land Rover. She checked that Lionel's saddlebags were there. She couldn't wait to see his face when she gave them to him. He must come with them on the picnic ride to find the new den. He spent so much time helping at Penyworlod and was so useful to Megan and Ian that she hoped they could spare him and let him borrow Ning. She plonked herself down beside Josh. At last they were off.

"What animal goes to bed with its shoes on?" Josh asked. "A horse," he said not waiting for a reply.

"Ha, ha," said Mory.

"OK, OK. There was a man who wanted to work at some stables and the owner said, 'Can you shoe horses?' 'No,' said the man. 'But I can shoo flies!'" Mory shrugged but Cara grinned.

"Got any more?" she asked.

"Oh, no, please not another one," said Mory.

"This is a good one," said Josh. "How do you get down off a horse?"

"It's obvious," said Cara, wondering where the catch was.

"You can't. You get down off ducks. Great jokes, eh? Felix told me them. He's got a book."

"Oh, no," cried Mory. "Save us from Felix's book." She stopped listening and looked through the tiny window at the front of the trailer. Used to travelling, the ponies' ears flopped placidly this way and that. Satisfied they were content Mory imagined cantering to a large log, beyond which the land fell away sharply. She and Dancer flew over and down, then up a steep hill to jump a hedge into a vast field where they galloped and galloped. Yes, she would do that and more.

"We're here," Cara announced as they turned into

the Penyworlod car park. Mory grabbed the saddle-bags and tumbled from the Land Rover.

"Won't be a minute," she cried, dashing off.

"Now where's she gone to?" asked Aunt Olwen, going to put down the front ramp.

Mory found Lionel in Ning's stable tacking her up.

"Lionel," she puffed. "Are you doing the cross country? Great." He grinned at her. Outside the stable was a new sign. EVENING SERENADE it said in black letters.

"Hey," said Mory. "Ning's got a sign. Does that mean she's staying?"

"Looks like it," said Lionel. He pulled back the door and came outside, putting down a grooming box.

"Pressie," said Mory. "These are for you." She thrust the saddlebags into the astonished boy's hands. "We've got to celebrate getting them by going on a picnic ride and finding a new den. Please ask Megan if you can."

"Mory…" Lionel held out the bags as if he couldn't possibly accept them, blushing to match the roots of his flaming hair. "Mory, I can't."

"You can't refuse a present, so there." Mory started to go. "No more polythene bags, eh?" Then she ran back to the car park. She'd have to hurry now or she would be late getting ready.

Lionel turned the bags over, assessing their usefulness. Ben trotted over to sniff his master's present. Lionel ran a hand absentmindedly over Ben's shaggy lurcher head.

"These are good," he said, a slow smile spreading. He could see how really useful the saddlebags would be. Just then Caroline Spencer brushed rudely past him, Mr Spencer following. She was beating a black and red jockey silk against her leg.

"I'm sorry love, it was the only colour left in the tack shop. It'll have to do for now." Lionel ducked back into Ning's stable. Ben followed him.

"Well, I hate it."

"You don't have to wear it."

"I do. I'll look stupid without one."

"May I remind you it was you who left the yellow and blue silk at home."

"Shut up," screeched Caroline, running off in a huff. Lionel peered over the stable door, wondering how Caroline got away with it. For a performance like that, his dad would have knocked him into next week.

FOUR

Cross Country

Mory counted eleven riders in the yard for the cross country schooling class. Caroline Spencer was late. They'd left her creating a flurry in the car park. Usually she was ready on time although Mory would rather she hadn't turned up at all. She felt haunted by her and was still uneasy about the incident with the mountain bike, half expecting some kind of retaliation. Mory pulled at the chinstrap of her skull cap and straightened the peak of her silk. She felt self conscious of her red and black stripes and her body protector was tight. They had to wear them in case they fell off but it was going to be hot with all the extra padding.

"Better to be safe than sorry," Aunt Olwen had told her when, groaning, she had zipped herself into it. She didn't mention that she had already fallen off loads of times and hadn't hurt herself for it crossed her mind that she might just have been lucky.

Lionel rode over on Ning.

"Ta for the saddlebags, Mory." He grinned shyly. "Be useful."

41

"Have you asked about the picnic ride?"

"I will," he said. Mory restrained herself from urging him to do so now. Megan and Ian were busy organizing the class but she did want to make plans.

Aunt Olwen waved goodbye. She had unhitched the Land Rover and was off to the shop in Llantrist to buy stores.

"I'm really looking forward to this," Mory said. "It's exciting and scary at the same time." She shook her wrists as an example of how trembly she felt, causing Dancer to wake up and wonder. "Sorry, pony." She pulled a face. "Shouldn't have done that."

"Can't say you don't give Dancer things to think about," said Lionel.

"What's going to happen?" Mory asked.

"There's to be two groups. Beginners and better," said Lionel. Mory was disappointed.

"You'll be in the other one then," she said.

"Not with Ning, I won't," said Lionel. "I'll be in beginners alongside you and Josh." Mory was glad. She felt more confident when Lionel was around. She could ask him questions she would feel silly asking Megan or Ian. Questions she often thought she ought to know the answer to. Like what happens if you land and drop your reins.

"Pick them up quick to get in control again," had been Lionel's reply to that one. Obvious really and she would have felt stupid asking that in front of

Caroline Spencer. But once she'd imagined a mishap she worried about it.

Now Ian was calling out the names of his group.

"Mory and Josh Harper, Caroline Spencer." He looked around for Caroline. She came running across the yard leading Doughnut at a trot.

Mory noticed that she was wearing a jockey skull cap like her own, with exactly the same black and red coloured silk, and not the usual black velvet hat. Mory's cheeks reddened. She didn't want anything the same as Caroline's and was tempted to take her silk off.

"Caroline, you're with me," said Ian. "So is Belinda Reed, Emily Richardson and Lionel Jones. The rest of you are with Megan. OK, at a walk my lot, follow me."

They set off and Ning decided this was going to be incredibly exciting. She jogged sideways doing a good imitation of a pony on springs.

"Behave yourself," growled Lionel. Unbothered, he turned Ning in a circle to come up behind the others. "Think you're going racing. Well, you're wrong." Ning's behaviour was infectious and Mory suddenly found Dancer coiled up underneath her ready to take off. Instantly she forgot her own excitement and concentrated on calming her pony. Everyone else's ponies seemed to take entering a field as part of a day's work and went placidly up the hill to the log jump Ian was indicating.

"We'll start with this," said Ian. "It's on a slight slope and we'll jump it going up the hill."

Mory began to feel easy. Jumping a log up hill or down hill was something she was used to. She was going to enjoy her morning if the jumps were no more of a problem than this.

"But first," said Ian, "we'll warm the ponies up. Lionel take the lead. Follow on behind him Caroline, Josh, Emily, Mory then Belinda. Make a large circle, Lionel."

Trotting round and having to concentrate focused Mory on her pony. The circle was large enough for Lionel to canter round and catch up the last pony. Each rider took it in turns to do this when Ian said go. When Mory cantered Dancer there was nothing but the thud of hooves on the grass, the contact of the reins, her feet reaching into the stirrups and her legs guiding and telling. It was a wonderful feeling as her pony responded. By the time they had gone round in a circle the other way doing the same thing Mory was more than ready to jump the log and so was Dancer.

Ian explained that he wanted each rider to canter in a circle and take the jump going up the slope and to keep cantering on the circle until he said stop.

"You're aiming for impulsion, balance and rhythm," Ian said. "In other words you need to have plenty of energy under you but at the same time you must keep your pony balanced by riding a careful straight pathway to the jump in nice plonkety, plonkety rhythm," he said. "Now Ning here is not very experienced but Lionel is so he's going to give us a demonstration. Off you go, Lionel."

Lionel blushed under his crash cap and set off. Out of the corner of her eye Mory saw Caroline purse her lips together, irritated, Mory suspected, by yet another instance of Lionel's good horsemanship being put on display. Mory glued her eyes to Lionel and wished the jump well. Lionel trotted Ning in a wide circle, broke into a canter and, turning on a gentle curve, brought the pony into the log on a straight line. He had everything just right, Ning was going forward in a balanced rhythmic canter and was urged into the air. Over she went and with a careful recovery Lionel took her round into a wide circle until Ian said trot and walk.

"Good girl," said Lionel, patting her neck. "Good girl."

"Nice jump, Lionel," said Ian. "What did she feel like?"

"A bit sticky. First time in the field," replied Lionel but he looked pleased.

Next went Belinda on Cassie. The pony popped over the log as did Emily on Toffee. Both ponies belonged to Penyworlod and had jumped the log many times.

"Josh next," said Ian. "Steady, Josh, remember what I said about balance and rhythm." There was no doubting Josh's determination. He was going to get Rustler over the log come what may. He needn't have worried. Rustler was as keen to jump it as his rider and sailed over.

"Josh, Rustler likes jumping," said Ian as Josh came trotting back. "It's your job to put him in a position so that he can jump with ease. Think about the line of your approach, Rustler's balance and keeping the rhythm. Which means don't rush." Josh was grinning from ear to ear and Mory suspected he hadn't heard a word.

"Caroline next," said Ian.

Caroline trotted off on Doughnut. She came round in a circle still trotting and asked for the canter rather late. It meant Doughnut was lacking in that important ingredient, impulsion.

"Push on," commanded Ian. Caroline kicked half

heartedly for two strides but gave up on the final three. The result was that Doughnut stopped with her nose over the log.

"Neither Doughnut or I believed you wanted to jump," said Ian going over. "Did you?" Caroline looked confused.

"It was Doughnut, she just stopped."

"No, you let her," said Ian. "Look, it's a good solid jump. Doughnut can clear this without thinking but if she's feeling lazy or that you don't want her to she can just as easily not bother. Bring her round again and tell her she's going to jump. Mean it this time."

"Yes," said Caroline, swinging Doughnut round for another go. Mory knew Caroline would hate to fail. But Caroline must have conquered her nerves for Doughnut came at the jump with more conviction the second time.

"Go on," said Caroline and Doughnut popped over the log as if it was nothing.

"Well done," said Ian. "You mustn't let her stop like that again. You don't want it to become a habit." He turned to Mory. "Last but not least," he said with a quick grin. Mory was glad to get going and trotted away from the others already plotting her route to the log.

"Come on girl," whispered Mory. "This is going to be fun." They cantered in a circle, turning on a gentle arc to face the log. Mory urged Dancer up the slope, saw the stride and pushed the pony forward. Dancer's ears pricked as they always did before a jump and then they were in the air, landing on the other side and recovering neatly before cantering away to the left in a big circle. Mory was pleased. There had not been a glimmer of hesitation.

"Well done," she said, stroking Dancer's neck. "Well done!"

"Good jump," called Ian. "You can bring her back now."

They did not jump the log going downhill. Ian moved them on up the field to where a stone wall divided one pasture from the next. At one point in the wall the stones were lower than the rest with two rustic poles on top making it up to the same height. Ian removed the two poles. Next he walked further along the wall to where there was a break in the stones. Again rustic poles made up the fence and underneath the poles was a ditch. Ian took out the top two poles leaving one remaining over the ditch.

"This time," he said, "I want you to jump the wall into the next field and canter round the jump in the middle of the field." Mory looked to see a kind of mound with a platform on the top. "Then back to the wall where you will jump the ditch. After the ditch I want you to canter down the hill, to swing round at the bottom and come back up the hill and over the log."

A shiver of excitement ran up and down Mory's spine. The jumps were all low but different from anything Dancer had been asked to jump before. Lionel was to go first on Ning. Mory watched with bated breath. What would Ning do?

Lionel cantered in a circle and rode straight at the wall, giving Ning plenty of time to look at it. She sailed over. They cantered steadily round the platform jump and turned back up the field for the ditch. Again Lionel came in straight, giving Ning a good chance to look at the ditch as he urged her forward. Her ears flickered once with hesitation but Lionel pushed her on. Ning put in a huge jump and cleared it with masses of room to spare. On down the field to the bottom where he turned in a gentle half circle and came back up. Ning popped over the log and cantered in a circle before Lionel let her come down to a trot and a walk. He was full of praise for her. She knew she had done well and put in a little buck of delight which set Lionel grinning.

"Good, Lionel," said Ian. "Next."

They went in the same order as before. This time Josh was less manic and took Rustler at a steadier pace and he went well. Josh was chuffed. Mory knew by the pink cheeks and huge grin. Even Caroline rode positively, trusting Doughnut more. When it was her turn Mory set off steadily in a careful circle, placing Dancer straight at the wall. Dancer showed no hesitation and was over it and across the field to the platform jump. Suddenly Mory realized that Dancer had no intention of going round the jump but meant to go over it, and to pull her away at the last minute

would unbalance her.

They both eyed the platform, coming to it at a steady canter. Dancer, not being quite sure what it was, did a big bound on to it and off again. Fortunately for Mory she was leaning well forward, otherwise she would have been pitched right out of the saddle. Flustered, she turned Dancer in a big loop for the ditch. She steadied her as they went up the hill. It was only when they were close that Dancer saw the black trench under the pole. She made to veer off but Mory was ready for evasion. She kept the pony straight and put her legs on hard. Feeling her rider's determination Dancer flew over the jump, like Ning, putting as much space between her and the ditch below as possible. Down the hill they went, Mory panting with the effort of keeping Dancer steady. They turned for the log and popped over it as if it was nothing.

"Good girl," said Mory. "Well done."

Mory arrived back at the others feeling contrite but before she could explain her error Caroline's penetrating tones filled the air.

"Trust you to show off, Mory Harper."

"It was a mistake," Mory said. "Dancer took me by surprise. She wanted to jump the platform. I didn't want to yank her away so I let her. I'm sorry."

"Decide who's in charge, Mory," said Ian. "It should be you."

"Yes," said Mory, bowing her head. "I didn't realize she was so keen to jump."

"She's keen and confident," said Ian. "You must make sure she stays that way by keeping her out of trouble." Mory nodded. "But you went into the jump just right. Well done!"

They moved down the field to the stream at the

bottom. Here Ian led the way to where the water widened into a pool and the ponies were expected to jump from a ledge into it. The ledge was only about fifteen centimetres above the water but the overhanging trees above the stream and thick undergrowth on either side made it gloomy.

"The ponies may not like coming into this. Give them time to see where they're going. It looks spooky in there and they've got to land in water. But they can see their way out on the other side. Positive riding is required. Take your time. No rushing."

Lionel had a bit of trouble persuading Ning to jump into the water but she went at last and, when she came out into the field on the other side, was rewarded with a mint. Josh had no problems, neither did Belinda or Emily.

When it was Caroline's turn she rode Doughnut towards the drop at a trot. From the corner of her eye Doughnut saw two mountain bikes speed recklessly down the hill towards her. She whipped round to get a better look and Caroline flew over her shoulder to land with a splash in the middle of the stream. The bikes skidded to a halt and Doughnut took off up the field, reins and stirrups flying.

"For goodness' sake," bellowed Ian. "What on earth do you think you're doing?" He jumped into the water to see if Caroline was all right.

From the other side of the stream Josh caught sight of Mory's alarmed face between the branches. It was the cousins. He'd seen how fast they had come down the hill. He shook his head.

"The nutters from hell!"

"Too right," said Lionel, steadying the prancing Ning, who had been set going by Doughnut's galloping hooves.

One twin stood frozen with a hand across her mouth.

"Sorry," said the other. "It was the hat. We thought you were her."

"What's that supposed to mean?" asked Ian. "That you meant to frighten the pony? Pick up those bikes and go back to the yard. Wait for me there." The twins pouted.

"Don't just stand there, move. Nobody gave you permission to bike in the fields. You may not think what you've just done is serious but let me tell you that that kind of irresponsible behaviour with horses could end up with someone getting seriously hurt." Unwillingly, the twins did as they were told. Ian pulled the wet and tearful Caroline from the water.

"Looks like they've ruined our jumping class," muttered Mory. She was longing to try Dancer over the stream.

Megan hurried over with the members of her class to see what had happened.

"We'll join forces," she called across to Ian. "Mory, jump Dancer over and we'll carry on together until Ian gets back."

Ian gave a wave and put his arm round the shaken Caroline. On the way back up the field he collected Doughnut and took pony and rider back to the yard.

Mory and Dancer were the only ones left in the field. Dancer wanted to join the other ponies and jogged to go. She jumped the drop with no urging, splashed through the water and trotted up the bank on the far side. Mory was extremely pleased.

When the class was over and they were riding their ponies back to the yard they discussed what had happened.

"Caroline was lucky not to be hurt," said Cara, sympathetically. "She must have hated falling off like that."

"You know what," said Mory. "The twins thought Caroline was me. One of them said something about us having the same hat. They meant me to fall off. Instead Caroline got the soaking."

"Right," said Lionel. "Her dad only got her that silk this morning. She moaned about the colours."

"Really?" said Mory. "That proves it. The twins wouldn't have known Caroline had a silk that colour."

"You've got to watch out, Mory. What Ian said is true. People can get hurt riding, especially with maniacs like them twins about."

"Maybe they'll realize now," said Cara. "Perhaps not knowing about horses they didn't realize how easily they can be upset."

"Perhaps," said Mory. But there was a wildness about the twins as if they had never been told no or never took no seriously. It left Mory feeling strangely unsettled.

"I think we've got to really look out for them. Keep on our guard. I don't think they would stop at anything once they got going."

Cara stared at her cousin. "Are you sure?"

"I agree with Mory," said Lionel. "They're dangerous."

FIVE

Plans

There was no sign of the twins or Caroline when
Mory and the others rode into the yard at the end of
their cross country lesson.

"Good riddance," thought Mory, though she did
feel a little sorry for Caroline. Aunt Olwen was back
from her shopping trip waiting for them.

"Had a good time?" she asked.

"Brilliant," replied Mory, sliding off Dancer and
running up her stirrups. She loosened the pony's
girth and reached into her pocket for some peppermints. Dancer munched her reward gratefully.

"Did you find out when Lionel can come on the
picnic ride?" asked Josh, dismounting beside her.
Rustler smelt peppermint and started nuzzling. Mory
handed Josh a couple.

"Well?"

"I don't know when. Lionel's asking Megan if he
can take Ning."

"What's this?" asked Aunt Olwen, overhearing.

"We want Lionel to come with us on a picnic

57

ride," said Cara. "So we can try out our new saddlebags."

"Well, try and pin him down to Thursday. I'll have time to collect him that morning."

"What about tomorrow?" asked Mory, wanting to go as soon as possible.

"Not tomorrow, Mory," said Aunt Olwen. "It's market day in Aberdawl. Glyn's putting some lambs in the sale. I'm giving a hand."

"Thursday, then," said Mory. "I'll tell him."

Lionel was in Ning's box rubbing her down.

"Thursday," he nodded.

"Can't you ask Megan now?" urged Mory. "Then we can arrange with Aunt Olwen what time to pick you up." Lionel grinned.

"If I don't I'll be dead, I can see that."

"Dead or mincemeat," said Mory. "We've got to find a new den, a secret place where no one but us will know where it is. That means somewhere secret for the ponies too."

"We might be lucky," Lionel said, fastening the stable door behind him and going in search of Megan.

Mory retrieved Dancer from Cara and, following the others, led her round the back of the indoor school to the car park. There was no sign of the Spencer's trailer. Caroline and Doughnut must have been taken home.

"Where are the twins?" asked Mory.

"They've been banned from Penyworlod," said Josh.

"Ian told Aunt Olwen. He's steaming mad with them."

"Not surprising after what they did," said Mory.

They were closing up the trailer's back ramp ready to leave when Ben came scampering over to greet them, tail wagging, his wet tongue licking any bit of skin he could find.

"Oh, Ben!" said Mory, wiping her nose. "Do you mind."

"Megan says Thursday is fine, Mrs Williams," said Lionel shyly. "I can have Ning all day."

"Good," said Aunt Olwen. "Will it be all right with your father?"

Lionel nodded. "He don't mind. I does my bit with the hens when I'm not helping here."

"Pick you up at half past eight then," said Aunt Olwen with a smile. "But I think you should tell him that you're going on a picnic."

"OK," said Lionel, who had no intention of doing so. His father was not keen on anyone having fun. He could easily say no and have him mucking out hen sheds instead. He only let him come to the Penyworlod Equestrian Centre because it was work. Lionel was sure his father would stop him straight away if he knew how much he enjoyed it.

He gave a wave as the trailer drove out of the yard. Mory and the others waved back. Just as they bumped through the gateway Ben broke away from Lionel and ran down the drive after them.

"Go back, Ben, silly dog," shouted Mory. But she

needn't have worried. At the Penyworlod entrance Ben turned and raced away along the drive.

"He was just seeing us off," said Josh. "Ben is a very polite dog, you know." Mory laughed, feeling good about life. The cross country session had gone well in spite of the twins and now they had an excursion on Thursday to look forward to. She knew exactly where she wanted to find a den. She hoped the others would agree.

"Shall we tell Aunt Olwen what happened to Caroline Spencer?" she whispered. Cara shook her head.

"If we tell Mum, she might not think the picnic on Thursday such a good idea. I mean we could meet the twins on their mountain bikes or something."

Josh agreed. "Don't say a word," he said. "Better they don't know we've got enemies. They'll never let us do anything if they know that." Mory was silenced immediately by the thought of constraints on her freedom.

"We mustn't let the twins get in the way of us having a good time. Anyway, after today the chances of them being allowed their bikes will be zilch."

"Dead right," said Josh. "If we'd done what they did our bikes would never appear again. If we had bikes, that is."

"Anyway," said Cara. "None of us would scare a pony like that on purpose."

"Still," said Mory giving it careful thought. "Even

if they are allowed their bikes, there's miles and miles of hills. We're hardly likely to bump into them, are we?"

As soon as they arrived back at Llangabby Farm all Mory wanted to do was to hurry through her chores. She still had loads of pots to pack for David and wanted to get them finished before Thursday. She was leading Dancer down the track for Black Rock ages before the others. By the time Cara and Josh arrived with Rustler and Misty, Dancer was ready to go out in the paddock.

"Mory, Mum says to remind you no riding tomorrow afternoon as Bob the farrier is coming," said Cara. Mory had quite forgotten and looked at Dancer's feet with new interest. The clinches had risen on the side of her hooves and although the shoes weren't much worn the hoof had grown. Mory gave her pony a pat.

"You're going to get your toenails cut tomorrow," she said, then led her across the yard to the paddock gate. Swinging the gate open she rummaged in her pocket for a handful of pony nuts, and slipped off the halter.

"Good girl," she said, giving Dancer the nuts and a pat. "We'll do some showjumping practice in the morning before Bob comes. How about that?" Then pulling the gate closed she hurried to the cowshed to get on with David's packing.

By Wednesday night Mory was in a welter of excitement about the picnic ride. She also felt a sense of achievement, having packed and labelled all David's pots. She and Dancer had had a good jumping practice in the morning and in the afternoon, while the others waited for Bob the farrier, she had walked out to Hill Farm to tell Felix about the picnic ride. When she got there no one had been in so she had left a note. By the time she had returned Bob had taken the shoes off all three ponies, cut and filed their feet and put them back on again. He'd given strict instructions to keep putting on the hoof grease. Mory did it religiously every day, like cleaning her teeth. It was such a dry summer and the last thing she wanted was for Dancer's hooves to crack.

"So what are you taking on this picnic?" Sheila asked when Mory finally flopped down at the kitchen table for her supper on Wednesday evening.

"I don't know," said Mory. "But lots. We've got huge saddlebags. So we can get loads in."

"Just because they're big," said Sheila, "doesn't mean you have to fill them."

"Mum, you know what I mean." Mory picked up her fork and prodded the food on her plate. "What's this?"

"Moroccan baked chicken with chick peas and rice," replied Sheila.

"Why?"

"Mory, stop poking it and eat. Where are the others?"

"It's foreign," Mory warned, when Josh plonked himself down beside her.

"Smells nice," he said. "What's it taste like?" He shovelled in a mouthful and chewed. "Nice."

"One satisfied customer at least," said Sheila. "David," she called from the back door. "It's on the table."

"It's not one of our chickens, is it?" asked Mory, suddenly alarmed.

"No, it came from the supermarket," said Sheila.

"And what's this yellow stuff?"

"Pepper."

"Why couldn't we just have had chicken casserole?" Mory asked.

"That's exactly what it is," said Sheila. "It has a fancy name, that's all. Just eat it." Mory tentatively eased a forkful into her mouth. It tasted all right and she chewed thoughtfully whilst listing some of the things she would take for the den. They would need to be packed and ready by tonight. A sudden and sharp flavour hit her taste buds.

"Yuk," she said and prized the offending morsel from between her teeth. "What's that?"

"An olive," sighed her mother.

"It's disgusting." Luckily David came in that moment.

"Any spare olives, give me," he said. "Love 'em." Mory carefully picked her way through her plate extracting five more and handed them over.

"I don't suppose you'll be wanting the jam tarts I made specially for your picnic either," said Sheila with a wicked glint in her eye.

"Oh, Mum," said Mory. "We will. We will really."

Sheila laughed. "I suppose I knew in my bones that Moroccan baked chicken with chick peas and rice was not going to be a hit with you, Mory."

"Jam tarts can be my hit," said Mory. "Can I have one for pudding?"

After supper Mory sat upstairs at her table with a list in front of her, chewing the end of her pen while she vaguely eyed the pictures and photographs of Midnight Dancer on her wall. She sighed and wondered if she had remembered everything. She had boiled eggs for sandwiches and there were loads of jam tarts. Whether they would survive being banged about in saddlebags was another matter. But even in bits they would taste good. She also had on her list hoof pick, halters, matches, rope, baler twine, torch. Then there was that old blanket of Lionel's which she had been keeping safe for ages. That might come in useful. Her saddlebags lay on top of her bed and stretched alongside them was Splodge. It was nearly bedtime but Mory thought she'd check things with Josh.

On her way to the door, she bent down and gave Splodge a stroke.

"Lovely puss," she cooed. He purred. Then she crossed the landing to Josh's room. She knocked on the door and pushed it open to find Josh with his nose in a joke book.

"Have you heard this one?" he said.

"No jokes," said Mory. "Listen." Reluctantly Josh put down the joke book. "Can you think of anything I haven't got down that might come in handy?" And she reeled off the list.

"Penknife," said Josh. "I'll bring my Swiss Army knife."

"Anything else?" said Mory, adding that.

"Food."

"We know about food."

"Peppermints." Although Mory had packets of mints everywhere she added them as well.

"That must be everything," said Josh. "I can't think of anything else."

"Neither can I," said Mory. She should have checked with Cara but Cara had disappeared after Bob the farrier had finished and had not been seen since. Too late to ring, thought Mory with a yawn and went downstairs.

In the kitchen Sheila was poring over a cookery book.

"I'm trying out a pudding tomorrow," she said when Mory came in. "More to your taste."

"Ah!" said Mory, understanding. "The Spencers are getting the Moroccan chicken thingy."

"I think so," replied her mother. "How does Hazelnut Apple Meringue sound?"

"Nice," said Mory, who liked meringue. She rummaged in the kitchen drawer for some matches, found a half burnt candle and took that as well.

"What are you looking for?" asked Sheila, turning the page of her book. "Mmm, baked treacle sponge. Might be a bit much after Moroccan chicken."

"This and that," said Mory. "Got any spare rope?"

"Rope? Ask Dad."

Mory wandered outside into the dusk. The sky was draped in black velvet and, in the west above the hilltop, streaks of orange glowed where the cloud frayed into tatters. A bat zig zagged across the yard, looping the loop before arcing above the barn roof and disappearing into the darkness. A fine day tomorrow, thought Mory with another yawn before crossing to the pottery.

"Got any rope I can have?" she said.

"What do you want rope for?" asked David, looking up from the bucket of glaze he was stirring.

"Not sure," Mory replied. Somehow rope just made her feel she had the right equipment. "I'm thinking of things for tomorrow."

"Big saddlebags and want to fill them?" David crossed to a box and rummaged until he found what he was looking for. "Here you are." He tossed Mory a brand new packet of sash cord. It still had the paper wrapper around it.

"Thanks, Dad."

"I want it back in good condition. It's to tie my boxes on to the roof rack when I go to London." David smiled. "Bedtime, love. You look done in."

"Night, Dad," Mory said, giving him a hug. He dropped a kiss on her hair.

"Night, night. Sleep tight."

Tucked up in bed with Splodge curled round her feet everything seemed just right. Tomorrow would be a wonderful day. They would find the perfect den, Mory knew it, and with that satisfying thought she fell fast asleep.

SIX

New Den

The following morning was sunny and bustled with the hectic activity that Mory loved. She had been awake early making sandwiches and packing her saddlebags. By the time Josh came out and Cara arrived from Llangabby, Dancer had been groomed until she gleamed.

Cara dumped her bulging saddlebags by the wall, grabbed a headcollar and went to fetch Misty. When she led him from the paddock she found Mory staring at the saddlebags.

"What you got in them?" Mory asked, curious.

"Food, bits and bobs, like hoof pick and halter, baler twine and stuff and swimming things. It's going to get really hot."

"Swimming things! We must take ours."

"Get mine too," shouted Josh as Mory dashed indoors. "Mory made a list but neither of us thought about swimming things," he informed Cara before turning back to pick out Rustler's feet.

Mory struggled back into the yard carrying two

sets of saddlebags. She leaned one set outside Rustler's stable and poked her head over the door.

"I've managed to stuff your towel and trunks in," she said. "The bags are really heavy now. They're going to bang like mad if we do lots of cantering."

"We won't be able to," said Josh. "Not until the ponies get used to them." Mory dumped the other set of saddlebags outside Dancer's stable, then looked into the next stable to see how Cara was getting on.

"It's no good hurrying me," said Cara. "I'm not nearly ready."

"I didn't say a word."

"You didn't need to. When you loom like that I know you're ready. Well, I'm not."

"OK, OK," said Mory. "Can I help?"

"You can get me some breakfast."

"Josh," said Mory. "What do you want for breakfast?"

"Toast and honey."

"Toast and honey all right for you, Cara?"

By the time Mory had made a plateful of toast and honey the others had caught her up.

"Thanks, Mory," said Josh, grabbing a slice. The honey ran, so Josh caught the drips in his mouth.

"Yes, thanks," said Cara.

They sat in a line against the wall, munching. Finishing a mouthful, Mory looked towards the track.

"I hope Felix got the note I left."

"He'll be here," said Josh. "He hasn't got as much

to prepare as us. A bit of oil on his bike is not the same as grooming a horse."

"I'll take the plate in," said Mory, getting up. "We should tack up now. Lionel'll be down any minute."

It didn't take long to saddle and bridle the ponies and when Mory led Dancer out of her stable the saddlebags were in place secured to the D rings on the saddle with baler twine. Mory felt ready for a great expedition.

"What we need," she said, "are leather thongs. Twine knots are so difficult to untie."

"Put them on a list, Mory," teased Josh.

At last hoofbeats rang loud on the track and Ben came running into the yard wagging not only his tail but his whole back end.

"Hello, Ben," said Mory, giving him an affectionate stroke. "You are pleased to see us." Lionel turned into the yard on Ning. The pony strode across the yard with ears forward, curious as to whom she would meet.

"Hi, Lionel," said Mory. "Ning's looking good. Does she mind the saddlebags?" Lionel's saddlebags were also secured with baler twine but were not as full as any of the others.

"Doesn't seem to," said Lionel.

"I think we're ready," Mory said. She looked towards the house. "Shall we say goodbye to Mum and Dad?"

"Doesn't look like they're up yet," said Josh.

"No," said Mory. "Let's go then."

They quickly adjusted their girths and mounted. Lionel swung Ning round and they set off with a clatter of hooves across the cobbles with Ben bounding ahead.

"We will have to collect Felix on the way," said Mory. "Doesn't look like he's an early riser."

Too late, David hurried outside to say goodbye. He crossed the yard in time to catch a glimpse of the picnickers as they disappeared down the hill, their excited chatter growing fainter. Smiling, he went back indoors, leaving the faint dust pall to settle once more on the track.

Lionel led the way up to the ridge. They walked up, giving the ponies a chance to adjust to the extra weight of the saddlebags although they appeared not to mind them. Mory let Dancer go at her own speed and felt the pony stretch under her with the effort of climbing the steep path. Cara was right, it was going to be hot. The whole long summer's day stretched ahead and was the beginning of a real adventure.

As the steepness evened out they followed the sheep track that led them to Hill Farm. They passed the fallen oak and Mory had a twinge of embarrassment at the mistake of stealing Caroline's mountain bike. Looking up, she saw a thin spiral of smoke drift above the ridge from the chimney that was still out of sight. When Hill Farm came into view Mory saw Mrs

Ashfield's battered old Range Rover parked outside.

As they approached the house the front door opened and Hector strode to the gate jumping it with a bound. Ben rushed to greet his friend. They ran one after the other in a mad circle charging across the heather. Pulling a rucksack on to his back Felix tumbled on to the path. From the shed at the side of the house he fetched Star Rider III. Mrs Ashfield held the gate for him. By the time the riders reached the house Felix was on his bike ready to go.

"Sorry, I didn't allow myself enough time," he said. "I made my own picnic."

"He didn't listen to the wise and the old," said Mrs Ashfield. "I warned him. Still, you're all here now. Off you go and have a lovely time." She closed the gate.

"When shall I expect you back?"

"I've got to be at Llangabby at five o'clock," said Lionel.

"A bit before then," said Mory. "We'll come back this way."

They trotted on to the ridge, saddlebags bumping. To Mory's surprise Dancer didn't seem in the slightest bit concerned. They reached the path which would lead them to the forest and Mory reined Dancer in.

"Let's find a den in the woods," she said. "Trees keep secrets and I think I know where to look."

"Why not," said Lionel.

"Good idea," said Cara. "Then we'll be near the stream for swimming."

"Is Hector coming with us?" asked Josh, for the big dog was still with them.

"Grandma told him to," said Felix. "He wouldn't have otherwise."

The path was steep and twisty. The dogs rushed ahead, next the ponies carefully picked their way down and Felix followed, pushing his bike. At the bottom they trotted towards the forest gate with Felix speeding ahead with the dogs.

"Wait until we gallop," laughed Mory. "He'll never keep up with us then."

Already Ning wanted to race and cantered on the spot.

"Pack it in, horse," said Lionel, who had no intention of letting the pony get her own way. He sat calmly and soon Ning was trotting like everyone else.

When they arrived at the forestry gate they found Felix fiddling with the padlock and chain.

"It's locked," he said.

"It's a cheat," said Mory, dismounting. "The chain's hooked over a nail to make it look like it's locked. See." And she unhooked it. Once everyone was through Mory closed the gate and hooked the chain back on the nail. She swung herself into the saddle.

The forest road was bedded with sharp stones and they walked, not wanting to bruise their ponies' feet. Felix had no such thoughts for the tyres of his bike and sped ahead. In the distance they could hear the sound of a waterfall.

"Let's go beyond the waterfall," said Mory. "To higher up, away from the fir trees to the beechwoods."

"Do you know this way?" Cara asked Lionel.

"Na," he said. "It's too far for walking."

"What about your bike?" asked Josh.

"That old bone shaker? You must be joking. Now if I had one like his…" And Lionel gave Felix's mountain bike a wistful look. "You can fly rough ground on that."

As if to prove a point Felix disappeared over the brow of the hill.

"Let's catch him up," said Cara. "This bit's not so stony."

The ponies, glad to get going, set off at a cracking pace and they were soon cantering to the brow of the hill. The road wound round and on and up. Here the pine trees gave way to a wood of beech and the land to the right of them dipped into a steep valley. The waterfall was behind them now but every so often they glimpsed a thread of water weaving between the trees.

They slowed to a walk and let the ponies recover. Above them drifted the plaintive mew of a buzzard and Mory looked up to see the bird spiral into the blue and be joined by its mate gliding into the same thermal. There was another mew. It sent a shiver up Mory's spine. It was eerie and gave the woods a mysterious feeling. The others seemed to sense the same thing.

Lionel whistled for Ben. Felix and both the dogs were out of sight. He whistled again.

"Hell's bells," said Mory. "Where's Felix got to?"

"I hope he's not going to keep disappearing," said Cara.

Josh shrugged. "You know what's he like."

"About as predictable as a grasshopper," said Mory.

At last Ben came careering towards them, ears laid flat, moving at terrific speed. He flew past them and

circled round behind, panting and pleased with himself.

"At least he hasn't caught anything," said Mory.

"Ah," said Lionel. "But he will."

"Great," said Josh. "Roasted rabbit."

"We don't need rabbit," said Mory. "We've got sackfuls of sandwiches."

"I got spuds," said Lionel. "Roast and bake." Mory sighed. She could see that she wasn't going to win on this one. Lionel wanted a rabbit and Ben would catch him one. She just hoped she didn't have to see it happen. It was too horrible to think about.

"Let's go on," said Cara. "Felix and Hector are up ahead somewhere."

As if to prove her point Felix came spinning down the road with Hector lolloping along beside him. He braked sharply causing stones to fly and swung his bike round.

"Where've you been?" he said. "I thought ponies were fast."

"Not on stony ground," said Cara. "But we can keep up with you now."

They set off at a steady trot, hoofbeats ringing out between the trees to echo back from the rocks. Felix, caught unawares, pedalled hard to keep up. Not allowed to canter, the ponies were soon covering the ground with extended strides. Slowly the valley beside the road levelled out a little and the riders slowed to wait for Felix.

"If we come off the road here and go through the trees there," said Mory, "we can walk the ponies across that rocky bit so no one will see their hoof-prints. It might be the start of our secret place." She dismounted and lifted the reins over Dancer's head. Above the rock grew tall and craggy. "Come on, let's see what it's like." Mory led the way across.

Felix arrived, puffing hard. It had been a long hard pedal up the forestry road.

"We're going to take a look in here, Felix," said Cara. "For a den."

Winding her way beneath the tall beeches, treading the bouncy leaf mould, the silence and stillness gave Mory a thrill of excitement. The stream seemed to have disappeared yet as she walked round the high rock wall, distant water fell. Strange, she thought. She carried on round the rocks which grew from the slope below and towered high. Suddenly Ben shot by, startling Dancer. He was there one moment, gone the next.

"Where'd he go?" Lionel asked, catching her up.

"Somewhere round here," said Mory. And there was Ben, standing between an unexpected alleyway in the rock. With tongue lolling he seemed to be saying, come this way.

"Can you hold Dancer a sec," said Mory, thrusting her reins at Cara.

"Wait for me," said Lionel, handing his reins to Josh. Felix leaned his bike against a tree and hurried to catch up.

It was like going through a tunnel for the gap above closed eventually. Ben hurried into the gloom. Following him they came into a clearing. Mory gasped with surprise and Lionel stood in amazed silence.

"Wow!" said Felix when he saw where they were.

"It's a secret kingdom," said Mory. "Look, there's even a cave." It was as if she couldn't quite believe her eyes. A trickle of water ran down the rock to the side of the dark entrance where it gurgled into an underground gully. Felix scampered over to investigate.

"Be careful," warned Lionel. "Those places aren't safe."

"Be full of bats, I bet," said Felix. "I wonder if Grandma has found this one yet?"

"It doesn't look like anyone's been here in years," said Mory. "I've got a torch so we can look inside."

"If we had some rope," said Lionel, "we could run a tethering line along from the sapling and tie it round this rock."

"We have," cried Mory. "I've got loads. Do you think the ponies would come through the alleyway all right?"

"Don't see why not," said Lionel. "It's plenty wide enough."

"Oh, let's try," cried Mory. "This is going to make the best den in the world."

SEVEN

Going Underground

Mory ran back between the rocks. The others were waiting patiently, the ponies idly flicking flies with their tails.

"This is the place," she said. "Lionel and I'll hold the ponies while you go and look." She took Dancer and Misty's reins from Cara. "If you don't think it's just brilliant then I'll die." Lionel relieved Josh of Ning and Rustler.

"It's good," he said. "And secret. Go and look." Josh and Cara hurried into the alleyway. Mory watched them go in.

"The entrance is brilliant! If you don't know it's there you don't see it," she said.

"It's the way the rock goes," replied Lionel. "Just right."

"And it's got water for the ponies. Only I didn't think to bring a bucket."

"We'll manage," said Lionel, settling his back against a tree to wait while Ning leant her muzzle on his arm. He rubbed her face affectionately. "Soppy mare," he said.

Mory stared up between the solid beech branches, wanting to see if the rocks went higher than the trees, but the leaves blocked her view. She rubbed her face in Dancer's neck.

"What do you think about it, lovely pony?" she asked. Dancer blinked slowly. With nothing to do she was slowly drifting off to sleep. Mory smiled. "Lazybones."

"You know," said Lionel, weighing things up, "if we could get up to those rocks above the entrance we could have a lookout."

"That's what I was thinking. It's about the most perfect place we could have found and we did it just like that."

"Ah, that's Ben," said Lionel. "He's good at finding things is Ben."

"True," replied Mory. "Chances are no person would find it by themselves. We are lucky." She was beginning to get fidgety, thinking the others had had plenty of time to look. "Could we lead the ponies in?"

"Better wait," said Lionel. "First time in they should go one at a time. We don't want no accidents."

"I wish they'd hurry up."

Lionel was enjoying the solid feel of beech tree against his back. "We got all day," he said and blew gently at a stray wisp of Ning's forelock, enjoying watching it snake in the tiny breeze.

Mory sighed. "I wish I had your patience."

"You could learn."

"Mmmm!"

At last excited chatter heralded the approach of the others.

"Hurry up," said Mory. "I want to loosen Dancer's girth. I should have done it ages ago."

Cara and Josh took their ponies and they all set about winding up stirrups and preparing the ponies for a rest.

"Why don't we tether them out here while we make the den ready for them;" suggested Cara. "We've got to make somewhere in there to tie them up."

"So you like it then?" asked Mory.

"You bet," said Josh. "It'll be the best den ever."

"Hurry up, you lot," shouted Felix, leaping to fetch his bike. "I want to borrow a torch."

They untacked the ponies and tied baler twine round a tree for each of them and fastened the halter ropes to the twine. They carried the tack through the alleyway to the clearing and found Hector stretched out in a pool of sunshine while Ben sniffed his way along the edge of the rock wall that towered above them. They made a careful pile of tack and saddlebags and Mory rummaged for the rope David had lent, delighted there was to be a use for it.

"Who's good at knots?" she asked.

"Lionel," said Cara without hesitation. "I can only do a quick release one." Mory unwound the rope and Lionel took an end, stretching it in along to the jutting rock where he looped and knotted it. Mory pulled the other end to the sapling.

"That's great," said Cara. "Just the right height for tethering." And she tied four loops of baler twine along the rope.

"Where's the torch?" badgered Felix.

"Wait until we've settled the ponies," said Josh. "Then we can take a look together." Fed up, Felix spun a pedal on his bike.

"Won't be much longer," said Cara. "But we do need to offer the ponies a drink."

Lionel pulled out a polythene bag from one of his saddlebags and took it to the trickle of water by the cave entrance, arranging the bag so it collected the flow.

"Give us a hand, Felix?" he asked. "Hold this then we can bring the ponies over and see if they want a drink."

"Are we ready to fetch them now?" Mory asked.

"Seems like it," said Cara.

"Just stay like that, OK, Felix?" said Lionel. Felix didn't move but neither did he say anything. He was bored. He might stay or he might not. Mory could see the signs.

"Let's bring the ponies in," she said.

They decided Misty should lead followed by Rustler then Dancer. Ning, as she was the dizziest, should go last. She might not like the narrowness of the rocks but she wouldn't want to see her friends go through without her. It worked perfectly. Misty led the way in his usual calm manner, ears pricked as he was curious, but happy to go. Rustler was the same. Dancer was a little hesitant but with encouragement followed. Ning decided it was scary and backed away. But when Dancer disappeared she nearly knocked Lionel flying in her rush to catch up.

"Daft pony," said Lionel, hanging on. "Blooming stupid you are." She calmed down as soon as she caught the others up. Each pony was offered water and each pony refused.

"You can lead a horse to water but you can't make it drink," grinned Mory. Felix didn't find it at all funny. He let the water bag spill and stomped off to the cave.

"If you're not coming then I'm going on my own."

"No, Felix, wait," said Mory. "We are coming. Wait. Stop him somebody."

"How?" asked Josh. Felix had already been swallowed by the black mouth in the rock.

Mory tied Dancer to a piece of twine and hurried to her saddlebags. She had to look in both bags before she found the torch.

"Come on, quick," she said. "Let's get after him before he gets lost."

"Don't panic," said Lionel. "He can't get far in the dark."

The four of them reached the cave entrance. It was

high enough for them to walk upright but the darkness was blinding.

"Felix," Cara called. Her voice sounded muffled and when Mory finally managed to switch the torch on they saw they were in a tunnel. Slowly their eyes adjusted to the gloom.

"Where is the idiot?" snapped Lionel, his voice harsh. He was ruffled perhaps by Felix having done a disappearing act.

"Creepy," whispered Josh. "I wouldn't like it in here on my own."

They followed the narrow beam of the torch down the tunnel.

"Felix," called Cara again. "Felix." Her voice trembled with echo and rang out louder than she meant.

"Hell's bells," whispered Mory, shining her torch upwards. "It's a great big cavern."

From nowhere a spine chilling wail reverberated in their ears and Felix leapt in front of the torch beam, waving his arms and pulling a grotesque face. Cara screamed and the light went wobbly. When Mory next found Felix he was on the ground with Lionel on top of him pinning his arms.

"You stupid berk," Lionel said. "Pack it in." They froze, watching while Lionel got off Felix's chest and stood up, his face pale and drawn. "Caves aren't places for messing in. You want to watch you don't get yourself in trouble." With that, Lionel hurried for the daylight at the end of the tunnel. Hector brushed past

him and sniffed his way down to where Felix lay on the cave floor. Felix wiped his face with the sleeve of his sweatshirt and pushed Hector's enquiring nose away.

"What's up with him? Can't he take a joke?"

"Get up," said Mory. "Let's go back outside."

They walked back along the tunnel and outside into dazzling light. Blinking, Mory looked round for Lionel. He was searching for something inside one of his saddlebags. Mory switched the torch off and went to put it away. As she bent down she caught sight of Lionel's face. It was crinkled so that his freckles seemed smudged. Something was wrong. Maybe he hadn't liked being closed in like that in the dark. Felix had made her jump but she hadn't been frightened. Lionel had. She could feel it.

She didn't say anything, just asked, "Where's Ben?"

"Off following his nose. I'm going to try for a rabbit." He caught sight of Mory's expression. "I gotta do something, see."

"Yes," said Mory. "Yes, you go off with Ben. Ask Josh. He'll come with you."

"Ask me what?" asked Josh on his way over.

"Coming hunting?"

"You bet." Lionel stood up. Felix was throwing stones at the water trickling down the rock. His face was closed and sullen. Lionel went towards him.

"Want to come hunting with me and Josh? Hector might be good at it."

"Not fast enough," said Josh, jumping in.

"He is," said Felix.

"Want to bring him and see?" asked Lionel. Felix threw another stone but the sullen look had gone. He tossed his last stone in the air and caught it.

"OK," he said.

Cara joined Mory and gave her arm a squeeze.

"We'll build a fire," she said. "For the potatoes."

"With stones, mind," said Lionel.

"Definitely stones all around," said Mory. She gave Cara a nudge in return and they watched the boys go down the alleyway trailed by Hector.

"Phew," said Mory. "Nearly a punch up!"

"Felix is a twit," said Cara. "He really can do some stupid things."

"I just hope they don't catch anything, that's all."

Cara gave her cousin a sympathetic smile knowing how upset she got if anything was killed. In the distance Lionel whistled for Ben.

"Maybe they won't," she said. "Let's make the fire."

The ponies dozed while the two girls searched for stones and built a round fireplace near the cave entrance. It took eight large pieces of rock before Mory was satisfied.

"And this flat stone can take the spuds when they're cooked and too hot to hold," she said.

"Should we build Lionel a spit in case he catches a rabbit?" Cara asked.

"No! It's too horrible to think about. He can build his own spit. Anyway, I haven't got a penknife."

"Right then, let's get some·wood," said Cara.

"We'll get loads," said Mory. "We can store it in the tunnel for another time. You know that cave might be quite good in the winter. We could have fires in it. It's high enough for the smoke to go up and not choke us."

"Maybe," said Cara. "We need some dry grass and twigs to start the fire with. Let's get that first."

By the time they had gathered their firewood and laid the fire and Mory had dragged several large branches into the tunnel for future use, when she planned to bring a small axe so it could be chopped and piled, they were beginning to wonder where the hunters had got to.

"Let's light the fire anyway," said Mory. "We can get the potatoes baking."

"I don't suppose Lionel brought any kitchen foil?" said Cara.

"Honestly, Cara, of course he didn't. They're to bake in the ashes." Then Mory caught sight of her cousin's face.

"Just my little joke," said Cara, grinning.

"Oh, very funny."

Mory found the matches and lit the dried grass laid under the twigs. It spat into life and soon the twigs were alight, their flame licking the larger pieces of wood laid above. It didn't take long for there to be a roaring blaze. A drift of smoke rose up between the rocks. Mory's gaze followed it into the blue.

"It'll be the smoke that gives us away," she said.

"Ah," said Cara, wagging her finger. "It might say we're here but where is here? People have still got to find the way in."

"I'm going to climb up the rocks, to that flat bit and look out," said Mory. "Can you keep an eye on the fire?"

"Be careful," said Cara, watching her cousin swing herself on to the sapling, causing a rustle that woke the ponies. She swung from there on to a rocky ledge and moved on up, carefully choosing her footholds. Cara hoped she would be able to get down again.

Mory reached what turned out to be a convenient lookout platform and waved before peering into the woods. She was as high as the treetops and could see the forestry road sloping downhill to the bend and in the other direction twist round before the rock above her got in the way.

"It's a fantastic view," she called down. "From here you can see who's coming along the road." She watched for a while but no one came, not even the boys, so she decided to go down again. It took longer than going up as she had to feel for footholds but at last, she swung on to the sapling and jumped to the ground.

By now there were plenty of embers in the fire and Cara had loaded them with the potatoes she had found in Lionel's saddlebags.

"This is boring," said Mory. "Let's go and find them."

"We can't. What about the ponies?"

"They'll be all right for a few minutes. We won't go far. Let's take our swimming things in case we find the stream."

Reluctantly, Cara was persuaded at last.

"You're over cautious," Mory told her. "Nobody will ever find their way in and if they did why should they harm the ponies?"

"They might panic and pull back from the line." Mory looked at the four dozy creatures, nicely shaded from the sun.

"Come on, get your swimming things," she said.

As they came out of the rock alley they heard a dog bark.

"Hector," said Mory.

They ran between the trees leaping the under-growth down and down to where the barking and the sound of falling water grew louder. Panting, Mory stopped. She could hear shouts as well.

"This way," she said. Cara hurried after her. Between the trees they could see water tumbling from above. They burst into the open and found them-selves looking down on a large pool. The boys, yelling and splashing, were having a water fight. Hector barked at the pool's edge while Ben lolled across a

rock, watching the fun. Nearby lay a jumbled pile of clothes.

"Some hunters!" said Mory. "Shall we hide their clothes?" She was too late. Josh saw her.

"Hey," he called. "You can't come down here. We haven't got anything on."

"Tough," called Mory. "You'll just have to come out backwards. Besides it's your turn to look after the ponies. Cara and I have made the fire and got the spuds baking. It's our turn for a swim."

"Don't be a pig," yelled Josh. Lionel had gone bright pink under his freckles and even Felix looked nonplussed for once.

"Let them get out," said Cara, pulling Mory back between the trees. "We can get changed over here."

The boys had terrible trouble getting their clothes on over their wet skin. In the end they didn't bother with their tee-shirts. Josh and Lionel went yelping and yelling back up the slope, waving them like banners as they charged between the trees. Felix was last.

"It's a secret river," he gasped while Hector barked at his heels. "And it's icy." Then he too was gone with a war cry that ripped the air.

Mory and Cara came to the edge of the pool.

"Help," cried Mory. "It's freezing." She let herself slide in, gasping at the chill. She pulled in a deep breath and ducked under. The water was clear and green algae grew on the rocks at the bottom amidst bubbles from the waterfall. She came up for air.

"Come on in, Cara," she said. "It's bliss."

At the edge of the pool the water fell away over a shelf of rock but there was no real current. Besides, the stream that ran out was tiny. After rain it would be different but it hadn't rained for ages. Mory swam towards the waterfall, letting the water tumble over her. Even here it wasn't deep.

"Be careful," Cara called. But Mory didn't hear above the splashing. She swam back and pulled herself on to a rock.

"It's deep enough to dive in," she said. "Here

goes." She sliced through the water and came up with a splutter.

"Cara, are you coming in or aren't you?"

At last Cara slid in beside her.

"It's so cold," she gasped.

"You get used to it," said Mory. "Swim."

They raced each other round the pool until they were puffed out. By the time they pulled themselves out and sat recovering on a rock they were ready to put their clothes back on. They towelled themselves vigorously to warm up.

"I'm starving," said Mory. "I think it's picnic time." She pulled her Mickey Mouse watch from the pocket of her jeans and put it on. "Definitely time for the picnic. It's nearly two o'clock."

"Already," said Cara. "It's not much longer before we'll have to go home."

They were heading back up between the trees when a twig snapped and there was a rustle in the undergrowth.

"The shouts came from down here, I know they did," a voice said. Mory grabbed Cara's arm and pulled her behind a rock.

"What was that?" Another voice. Mory put her finger to her lips then cautiously looked out. Three figures veered away and disappeared between the trees. Her heart skipped a beat. One of them was Caroline Spencer and the other two were the twins, Phoebe and Trish.

EIGHT

A Near Miss

Once Caroline and the twins were out of sight, Mory and Cara raced from tree to tree, checking and rechecking that they weren't being followed. With a nod they dashed into the rock alley to arrive panting in the clearing.

"What's up?" said Josh, so startled he nearly trod on the sandwiches he was unpacking.

"It's them," gasped Mory. "Caroline Spencer and the twins."

"Where?" asked Lionel.

"Down near the pool. They heard our voices. They seem to have gone further into the woods but they're bound to come back this way." Lionel took a quick look at the fire.

"No smoke from that," he said. "But they got to be gone before we have the picnic."

"I'm going to climb up to the lookout," said Mory, swinging on to the sapling. "You can see the road from up there."

"Don't let them see you!" said Lionel.

"We'll stalk them like proper Indians," said Felix, setting off.

"Wait," said Lionel. "Let Mory take a look first."

"We must be careful," urged Josh. "They mustn't find our den." Reluctantly, Felix waited.

Mory crabbed her way up to the ledge and lay on her tummy. The trees were an impenetrable carpet but she did see three bikes lying near the edge of the forestry road.

"Talk about bad luck," she muttered. "They must have been going by when we were making all that row." She ran a hand through her damp hair. "Blow!" She wriggled backwards off the lookout platform and climbed down again.

"Their bikes are by the road," she told the expectant faces. "I think we should sit it out. They're never going to find us in here unless we give ourselves away."

"We must just make sure the dogs don't bark," said Cara.

"The dogs!" said Mory. "Where are they?" Hector was sitting alert near the fire noting the general panic but Ben was nowhere to be seen. "Right," said Mory, thinking fast. "We need a lookout to say when the bikes are gone and a search party to find Ben."

"Dratted dog," said Lionel. "He was here a moment ago. He must have caught a scent. When he does he's off."

"The important thing is to get out of here without

being seen. If they see us in the woods it doesn't matter so much."

"Best of all if they don't see us at all," said Josh.

Felix had been quiet throughout all of this and not really listening.

"Felix, do you want to be lookout?" Felix shook his head.

"Me Indian brave," he said. "Sleeping Cloud."

"Felix, this is serious," said Mory. "We've let you in on our secret den and we need you to help us keep it secret."

"Sleeping Cloud keep all secrets." Felix lifted a hand and with a solemn look made for the rock alley. Lionel raised his eyes and shook his head.

"Felix is off," whispered Josh.

"I'll do the lookout," said Cara. "Don't let Felix steal their bikes."

"Steal their bikes," said Mory horrified. "That would really give us away." And she dashed after him with Lionel right behind her.

"You sure about being lookout?" asked Josh. Cara nodded. If Mory could climb up there so could she and with the twins about there was no way she would leave the ponies.

"OK," said Josh and raced after the others. Cara swung herself up by the sapling and started to climb. She was concentrating so hard she didn't see Hector get up and trot off down the alleyway.

Outside the den the four of them fanned out, bent

low and hid themselves behind the trees. At first there was nothing and they wriggled forward. Lionel kept a special eye on Felix in case he did something stupid like leaping out or making whooping Indian calls. Then Mory saw movement a little further down the hill. She signalled to Lionel, who tapped Felix on the arm. Felix caught Josh's eye and pointed. Disgruntled voices drifted towards them.

"It probably wasn't them anyway." Definitely Caroline, thought Mory.

"I bet it was." Phoebe, Mory guessed.

"Caroline's right. It could have been anyone." That was the other twin, Trish. Mory peered cautiously between the undergrowth.

"If it was them, they'd be on their ponies. They're always on their ponies. I bet they go to bed on their ponies." Caroline's sarcastic tones were not difficult to recognize. Mory flushed with indignation and ducked down, holding her breath they were so close. Luckily there was no sign of Ben to give them away and from the corner of her eye Mory saw Lionel wriggle close to Felix ready to grab him just in case. But Felix didn't move a muscle. Mory breathed a sigh of relief watching the girls wind their way up between the trees until their grumbling became a murmur. Soon Cara would be able to see them from the lookout. With luck they would get on their bikes and go.

Mory was just beginning to relax when there was an eerie howl. Several yells and a scream followed and

three sharp barks came in reply from further down the valley bringing Hector's great grey shape ghosting between the trees.

"Now what's happened?" cried Mory.

"That's Ben down there," said Lionel as Hector disappeared in the direction of the barking.

"I think Hector's given us away," Mory said. She checked for signs of the girls returning.

"Talk about the hound of doom," said Josh.

Felix grinned. "He does that sometimes."

"Caroline and them twins is not to know that," smiled Lionel.

They hurried back to the den to find Cara almost

down from the lookout. She swung from the sapling, an impish grin on her face.

"What happened?" asked Mory. "Have they gone?"

"Oh, they've gone all right," said Cara, hardly able to contain herself. "Hector was sniffing about on the road and then let out this great howl just at the moment Caroline and the twins came out from the trees. They yelled and one of them even screamed. Then they ran for their bikes. You should have seen them go. They didn't notice Hector was wagging his tail. They never even looked back. I know I shouldn't laugh but it was the funniest thing I've seen in ages." By now they were all grinning.

"So Hector vanquished our foes," said Mory.

"There is one thing," put in Lionel. "What if they recognized him?"

"But they've never seen Hector. I'm sure they haven't. If it had been Ben, well, they'd have known we were around straight away. But not Hector, surely," said Mory.

"Never mind that, let's get the dogs and have our picnic," said Felix. "They've gone and I'm starving."

While Lionel and Felix went to whistle in the dogs, Mory took a stick and uncovered the rather burnt looking potatoes, hooking them on to the flat rock she had prepared as a cooling tray. Cara and Josh unpacked the rest of the picnic and Josh, who couldn't wait, stuffed an egg sandwich into his mouth.

"The jam tarts have survived pretty well," said

Cara. "They're a bit broken but most of them are still whole."

"These spuds aren't any good," said Mory. "They're completely burnt."

By the time Lionel and Felix came back with the dogs the food was laid out ready.

"Keep the dogs off," cried Mory. "They can have some left overs." The dogs were made to sit down well away from the picnic and kept hopeful looks on their faces until they realized they weren't getting any. Then they lay side by side and dozed.

Mory was quite right about the potatoes. Josh cut them open with his army knife and they were burnt right through.

"Thank goodness we've got lots of sandwiches," said Mory, tucking in. Lionel held back, disappointed that his potatoes were burnt. "Tuck in," said Mory, handing him a sandwich.

"And no rabbit," he said, lamely.

"A good thing too," said Mory. "Eat up, please." Deciding it was all right, Lionel took the sandwich and ate as if nothing had passed his lips for a week at least.

By the time the picnic was finished and the dogs had been given some jam tarts as a special treat it was time to put out the fire and pack up. They offered the ponies more water and tacked them up. By now it was getting late.

"Let's leave the tethering rope in the cave," said Mory. "I'll buy Dad some more. I bet Lionel's got some spare poly bags." In the end they left the matches, the half candle, loads of baler twine, Lionel's old blanket and the rope stuffed into two polythene bags which Lionel pulled from his saddlebags like a magician. Mory hid the bags in the tunnel behind the wood supply.

It was sad leading the ponies back down the rock alleyway. It had been such a perfect day, especially having escaped being discovered by Caroline and the twins. But there was great satisfaction in knowing that Hector had scared them off. Realizing they were going home, the ponies set off at an eager pace. Hoof-beats rang out and they were soon trotting down the forest road following Felix and the dogs who sped ahead.

By the time they arrived back at Hill Farm Mrs Ashfield was waiting by the gate.

"I was going to walk to meet you," she said. "You've beaten me to it. Hello, Hector." Hector pushed his nose into her hand and gazed up at her, his tail wagging in wide sweeps. Mrs Ashfield massaged his ears. "Good dog. Good boy." Then she looked at Felix. "Did you have a good day? Shall I rub your ears?" Felix pulled off his bike helmet.

"No thanks," he said. "With rubbing like that, they'd come off." He turned to the others. "It was a great day. When are we going next?"

Mory looked at Lionel.

"How about Monday?" she asked. "Could you get Ning?"

"Will Mum fetch her is the next question," said Cara.

"We'll let you know," said Mory. "We'd better not be late for Aunt Olwen. She might not fetch Ning again if we are."

They turned their ponies for home and trotted off towards the rock crop waving goodbye as they went. When they finally clattered into the yard at Llangabby they were met by Mab and her two wriggling puppies barking a welcome. Josh leapt off Rustler to say hello. Mab went behind the ponies eager to round them up.

"No, Mab," said Josh.

The trailer was hitched and ready to go so Lionel got on with untacking Ning. Aunt Olwen came out to give a hand.

"Had a good day?" she asked, although she could see by their faces that they had.

"It was lovely," said Cara.

"The best ever," said Josh.

"I'm pleased to hear it. Right, Lionel, let's get this pony loaded."

They waited until Ning was in the trailer before saying goodbye to Lionel and Ben, then they set off down the track to Black Rock leading their ponies. There was a whinny of dismay from Ning as she realized she was going off on her own. Dancer whinnied in reply.

Arriving in the Black Rock yard they untacked

their ponies. They left the saddlebags in a pile and carried the tack to the tack room. After a quick wash down Mory led Dancer to the paddock gate. Not many pony nuts left. She must remember to fill her pocket. She gave Dancer what she had as a thank you and let her go. The pony wandered off and was soon grazing contentedly.

"A happy pony," smiled Mory, going to collect her saddlebags and take them indoors.

Sheila was in the kitchen reading yet another cookery book.

"Did you make the pudding?" Mory asked.

"Oh, there you are," said Sheila. "It seems like Sunday is turning into quite a party."

"What do you mean?" asked Mory, suspicious at once.

"Did you have a nice picnic?"

"It was great, Mum. Really great. So who else is coming on Sunday?"

Sheila took a deep breath as the giver of bad news often does.

"I'm afraid it's Caroline and the twins. Apparently there was no one free to be with them and Mrs Spencer rang to say that they couldn't come. Naturally, I said bring the girls too."

"You said what!" Mory gasped. "That's just about the worst news I've had in my whole life." And with that she dumped her saddlebags on top of the cookery book and marched outside to tell the others.

NINE

The Terrible Twins

Sunday loomed large. Mory had been dismayed by Josh and Cara's reaction to spending an evening with Caroline and the cousins. Josh seemed more curious than angry and Cara went into *I will make the best of a bad job* mode.

"It's only for one evening," she said. "We can manage that."

"You might be able to," said Mory. "Being civilized to Caroline and those twins will just about kill me."

"No it won't."

Outraged, Mory had stormed off.

When it came to Saturday and their riding lesson Mory was not sure she wanted to go. To be faced with Caroline two days running seemed like an overdose. Cara tried persuasion but Josh had a better tactic.

"Fancy letting her get to you like that. You've let her win," he said.

Josh was right! Not going meant Caroline had triumphed. In the end she couldn't bear to miss the lesson, realizing it was silly to let Caroline stop her doing the thing she loved most. She arrived at Penyworlod prepared to put up with every single comment and could hardly believe her luck when Lionel gave her the news that Mrs Spencer had cancelled Caroline's lesson.

"I bet you're glad you've come now," said Cara.

"The first ever lesson without her," cried Mory.

It was an excellent lesson too. Liberated from Caroline's criticism, Mory enjoyed herself hugely. Dancer must have sensed Mory's mood for she was full of fun and jumped with energy and enthusiasm. Lionel watched them and at the end made a point of coming over.

"You and Dancer are like that, Mory," he said, clasping his hands. "Nice and together. I noticed in the cross country. It's coming good."

"Yes, she was great except for jumping the platform."

"That's her. Strong willed, given a chance," said Lionel. "Just as well you are too." He gave Dancer's neck a pat, looked up and winked. "Good luck for tomorrow night."

"You heard?"

"Cara told me. Give as good as you get, girl," he said. "Oh, and Mrs Williams has arranged Tuesday with Megan. I can have Ning all day again. Brilliant, eh?"

"You bet," said Mory. "We can really explore. I must remember to take a spare torch battery. I want to get a good look round the cavern." For a moment, Lionel's face clouded.

"I'm bringing a towel this time," he said. "For the swimming."

He's not keen on that cave, thought Mory. Not that it mattered.

When Sunday arrived Mory spent the morning with Cara and Josh, schooling Dancer in the Llangabby paddock, practising her over a Handy Pony course they made. The Llantrist show was only a week away and Dancer still snorted and shied at anything new.

"Perhaps, when she's met everything we can possibly think of that's different she'll stop it," said Mory.

"Next time we'll try my teddy bear," said Cara.

"And a pile of my Mogul Monsters," said Josh.

"Oh, thanks," said Mory. "Mogul Monsters will just about drive her insane." Josh grinned a wicked grin.

"I was serious," said Cara.

After they had taken the ponies down to the Black Rock paddock they were the three hungriest people ever to troop into the kitchen. Food there was in plenty, scattered everywhere, in different stages of preparation. Sheila looked at them in a vague sort of way.

"Lunch at Llangabby," she muttered, so they had to trudge all the way back up the track.

"I'm keeping out of Mum's way this afternoon," said Mory.

"We could ride up to Hill Farm and tell Felix about Tuesday," suggested Cara.

"Good idea," said Josh.

"I'm going to start Dad's birthday mural," Mory decided.

"When is it?" asked Cara.

"August 28th so I haven't got that long."

"You've got ages," said Josh.

"Maybe if I painted like you, blobs everywhere. Anyway, that's what I'm going to do."

"Fine," said Josh, not feeling in the mood for an argument. "Me and Cara can go to Hill Farm on our own."

"Waste of time when you can tell Felix tonight." Hunger was making Mory bad tempered.

After a good meal provided by Aunt Olwen Mory felt much better and when at last she sat at the table in her bedroom in front of a large piece of drawing paper she was enthusiastic about planning her design. Mory had long ago promised to paint David a Midnight Dancer mural on the white wall of his pottery. David had already bought her the paint, black for Dancer, yellow for the moon. It sat under her table and right now her feet rested on the tin of black. It would be a shame to leave it until the last minute and have to rush. She licked the end of her pencil and began.

Concentrating hard, Mory roughed out Dancer cantering, her pencil spinning across the page to make Dancer's mane and tail stream. Then she sat back. Somehow the proportions seemed all wrong. She sighed. It was going to be more difficult than she thought. She picked up her sketch book and set off for the paddock. Mrs Ashfield did it by studying animals in real life. So would she. She would sketch her pony in the flesh.

Dancer was snoozing in the shade of the oak tree. Mory climbed the gate, balanced herself on top and drew. By the time the others came clattering into the yard several pages were filled with assorted parts of Dancer's anatomy. She closed her book and hugged it to her. Sketching from life seemed to have helped.

"Did you see Felix?" Mory asked, jumping down.

"There was no one in," said Josh. "Guess who we did see?"

"Dunno."

"Caroline and the twins."

"They were really friendly," said Cara. "Weren't they, Josh?"

"It was weird. Too friendly if you ask me."

"They wanted to know where you were," said Cara. Mory shivered in spite of the sun.

"What for?" Cara shrugged.

"Dunno."

"Don't worry, we didn't tell them," said Josh. "Just in case they invaded Black Rock."

"They will tonight when they're invited," sighed Mory. "I'm not looking forward to it one bit."

As the evening drew near Mory found herself putting out the cutlery on the dining room table and carrying through plates. As there were now so many coming it was officially a party. When she had arranged everything and rather nicely, she thought, it was a shock to be told to go and change.

"Change!"

"At least into some cleaner jeans," said Sheila.

"Mum's taking this really seriously," Mory confided.

"I'd better change too," said Cara and set off for home.

Filled with anxiety and foreboding by the time her cousin reappeared, Mory hoped everyone else would arrive before the Spencers but this was not to be. The first car to bump down the track and turn into the yard was theirs. Mory saw it from her bedroom window where she and Cara were lurking until the last minute. It looked like the last minute had arrived. She took a quick peek at the big sketch of Dancer lying on her table. She would a thousand times rather be working on that. With a sigh she followed Cara to the stairs, took a deep breath and resolved to do what her mother asked – *make an effort*.

The pair of them listened to David ushering the guests into the living room.

"One, two, three, go," said Cara and went.

Mory forced herself to follow. Clump, clump, clump, clump. Her feet were like lead. All she wanted to do was run back to the safety of her bedroom. Aunt Olwen and Uncle Glyn arrived at the living room door at the same time as she did. Aunt Olwen gave her a smile and Uncle Glyn put a finger in his collar and pulled. He didn't look very comfortable either. She followed them in.

Caroline was perched on a chair holding an orange

juice, seemingly quite at home. The cousins were standing nearby, sullen and without drinks.

"Ah, good, Mory," said David spying her. "I'll leave you to look after the younger members of the party." He smiled. Mory stared back in a kind of trance. It was like a bad dream.

"Hello, Caroline." Picking up a handy bowl of crisps, she offered them. "Crisp anyone?"

"No, thank you," said Caroline. The twins stared stony faced.

"I'll have some," said Cara.

"Me too," said Josh, arriving at what he could see was a tricky moment. He and Cara both took a handful. Mory put the bowl back where she found it. She was unable to think of a thing to say.

"Caroline, why don't you introduce Mory to your cousins," said Cara.

"Why?" There was an uncomfortable pause.

"They haven't met properly yet."

"Phoebe, Trish, this is Mory Harpic smells like a carpet. OK?" Mory flushed bright pink.

"Uncool," said Josh and shook his head. Mory did her best to ignore it and turned to the twins.

"I'm pleased to meet you."

"Did someone speak?" asked Trish. Phoebe went through an elaborate sniffing routine.

"Or did they reek?" she cried and the twins fell about laughing. Caroline's smirk was triumphant. Something went tight in Mory's chest. She had to get outside. She turned round and rushed blindly for the door. Cara hesitated, then followed Mory out of the room.

"Did someone say something or what?" asked Caroline and the twins convulsed all over again. Josh gave up after that and went after the others. He ran upstairs but they weren't in Mory's room. Eventually he found them in the tack room. Mory was in a fury of rage and hurt.

"I try," she spluttered. "I really try."

"You do," said Cara. "I know you do." But there was no comforting her cousin.

A deep bark summoned Josh outside. Hector was sniffing something interesting outside the pottery and Mrs Ashfield and Felix were on their way indoors.

"Felix, over here," hissed Josh. "Quick."

Mrs Ashfield saw Josh and smiled.

"Stay, Hector," she said and went indoors leaving Felix to scuttle across the yard. Josh steered him into the tack room.

"What's up?" he asked. Mory sat silent on an upturned bucket.

"Caroline and the twins have been foul to Mory," Josh said. "The twins are making Caroline worse." He told Felix what had happened. "It's not fair, Mory can't say a thing in reply."

"Yuk," said Felix. "Let's get them."

"But how?" wailed Mory. "I'll have to put up with it. If I retaliate Mum and Dad'll just about kill me."

Felix wasn't listening.

"Get them out in the yard," he said. "I've had an idea."

"Whatever you're thinking, the answer is no," said Mory. She stood up. "We'd better go back in. They'll be wondering where we are."

Taking a deep breath, she marched out of the tack room and across the yard.

"At last!" said Sheila. "I sent Caroline and the twins up to your room to find you. I'm waiting to dish up."

"What? How long have they been up there?"

"I don't know," said Sheila. "Just fetch them." Mory needed no telling. She was furious. They'd have had a chance to pry into goodness knows what and her sketch of Dancer was still lying on her table. She charged for the stairs. When she opened her bedroom door Caroline and the twins, clustered round her table, started guiltily.

"Food's ready," said Mory and held the door wide for them. Without a word they trooped across the room and went past her on to the landing.

"Aren't you coming?" one of the twins asked.

"I need a tissue," Mory said. She was desperate to see what they had been up to. When she did see she let out a gasp. They had drawn all over her sketch. Dancer now had roller boots for feet, a pair of giant insect wings and a great beard. Underneath was written, "Midnight Mosquito bites in the night! The

only way to keep this insect moving is to put it on wheels." Her sketch was ruined and when she picked it up she found it was torn into four pieces.

"Right," said Mory. "That's it." Shaking with rage she hid the pieces under her bed and went downstairs. She did her best to pretend everything was normal although eating was impossible. She chased bits of Moroccan chicken around her plate while in her best secret agent manner told Cara what had happened.

"Keep them talking," she muttered, teeth clenched.

"What shall I say?"

"You'll think of something. Just keep them occupied and don't let them back upstairs." Cara did

her best, aware that Mory had gone into a huddle
with Felix and Josh. When it was pudding time Mory
handed Cara some hazelnut meringue in order to
whisper, "I'm going outside for a bit. When I come
back ask to show them the tack room or the pottery.
Anything. Just get them outside."

Cara was feeling horribly uncomfortable. The
grown ups seemed to be enjoying themselves,
laughing and chatting like anything, and here she was
having a revolting time. She fetched Caroline and the
twins a bowl of pudding each. They didn't even say
thank you. It was as if she didn't exist any more and
was talking to an empty space. All she had managed
to learn was that the twins went to boarding school
and thought ponies stupid. When she asked Caroline
why she had missed the riding lesson, Caroline stared
straight through her. It was a relief when, at last,

Mory poked her head round the door. She had quite run out of things to say.

"Want to look around outside?" she suggested.

"Why not," said Caroline. "It's boring enough in here."

The yard was deserted. The air carried the scents of evening and the sky was reddening.

"OK, now we're here, what are we going to look at?" said Caroline. "You're the host or at least Mory is, wherever she's got to. Let's look at the repulsive stables. You can smell them from here."

Caroline marched towards them when, to her surprise, Dancer's door burst open and she took the full brunt of a jet of water bang in the stomach. Next it was attack by bucket. Josh and Felix picked off a twin each. Caroline screamed and wailed but the twins quickly launched a counter attack. There was a fight for the hose pipe which Mory almost lost until Phoebe went for her own bucket and filled it in the trough.

Soon the yard was full of shouting, yelling water fighters, until the air, rent with one of Hector's great howls, brought them to a sudden and unexpected stop. Its echo died away and Felix put his dripping hand on the dog's neck to stop him howling again. The twins gawked at the big grey dog while David stood, a looming presence, outside the back door before bellowing into the silence.

"What on earth is going on here?"

Over the paddock gate three startled pony faces stared at the mayhem and Caroline started to snivel.

TEN

Ambush

Disgrace was hardly the word for it. Mory lay in bed while the whole ghastly evening replayed over and over in her head like an unstoppable film. Her parents had been livid. They might have got away with calling the water fight a game if Caroline had not wept and wailed and that was after she had joined in. Caroline had soaked her with at least one bucketful from the trough. To her surprise the twins had taken it in good part and Phoebe had even pulled a conspiratorial face behind her father's back when she was getting her incredible telling off. It was only a soaking for goodness' sake and everyone ended up wet. That appeared to be the disgrace. Soaking your guests was the height of bad manners. But it was the only part of the evening that had been any fun.

"Hell's bells," sighed Mory. Splodge crept down the bed purring. She ran her fingers down his silky fur and hoped, in time, she would be forgiven. For some reason everyone seemed to think it was her fault. She had tried to prove provocation by showing the ruined sketch but nothing she said made any difference. If anything it only made things worse. The upshot had been no riding for five days.

"I think I'll run away," she whispered into Splodge's fur. Then she sat up. That would show them. Then she lay down again. No, it was no good. She would have to try and make amends. Tuesday's trip to the den was cancelled and Lionel didn't get many opportunities to ride out in the hills. She felt terrible about that. And what about practising for the Llantrist show? Everything was ruined as she knew in her bones it would be.

She sat up again. She'd help with the clearing up and be so good they would see how sorry she was – except that part of her wasn't. She was glad to have soaked Caroline. Try as she would she couldn't be sorry for that. She'd have to pretend that bit of her didn't exist. Another sigh and she curled up with Splodge nestling under her arm and eventually fell asleep.

The next morning Mory was up early and, after feeding Splodge, she put the kettle on ready to make her parents' tea. Next she pulled out her mother's rubber gloves and began the washing up. There were glasses and plates everywhere. It was a real penance and felt like it would take a week at least. She was drying the first load on the draining board when David came into the kitchen yawning. She must have been a surprise for he looked startled to see her.

"What are you doing?" he asked.

"Clearing up," she said. "You can leave it all to me. I'm sorry ... I'm really sorry I spoiled your party. I didn't mean to and it wasn't all my fault. And what about the special ride Lionel was coming on tomorrow. It's not fair if we can't go on it. It wasn't just me, you know. Caroline started it." And to her surprise she flung down the teatowel and burst into tears. "Oh, hell's bells! I hate her. I really hate her," and she slumped on to the bench by the kitchen table.

David ran a hand through his hair and looked with concern upon his weeping daughter. Then he sat next to her and put his arms around her. Mory lifted her tear stained face to his.

"And she hates me. She hates me more than I hate her. At least I try and be nice. She never does. Never ever." Then she buried her face in her father's dressing gown and sobbed and sobbed. David squeezed. When the sobs stopped he pulled a tissue from his pocket and Mory blew her nose.

"What are we going to do with you?" David asked, shaking his head.

"Nothing," said Mory. "I'm going to make you tea and get on with the clearing up. It's part of my sorry. And I'll write letters apologizing to everyone, even Caroline, if I have to. Only we've got to be able to go on the ride tomorrow because of Lionel."

In the clear light of a new day David could see that there must have been two sides to the story. Last night, when he had been angry, it was true, he had directed most of his fury at Mory.

"Go on then, make some tea. I'll have a talk with your mum."

Mory looked at him gratefully.

"Just Tuesday. It doesn't matter about the other days." She swallowed. "Or even the Llantrist show."

After the tea, the clearing up and the millions of apologies she made, somehow, some incredible how, Tuesday was still on. Monday and Wednesday ended up being the only days riding was banned. There was also a list of chores to be done but Mory didn't care about them. She was overjoyed.

As they cantered along the ridge the following morning, the joy was still with her. How could it not be? The sun shone from a blue sky, the ponies were fresh from a day's rest, they had saddlebags stuffed with food, swimming things, a spare torch battery and the whole day ahead of them. The dogs lolloped alongside and Felix brought up the rear on Star Rider III getting tangled with the bucket he'd volunteered to carry over his handlebars. Nothing seemed to matter, not Caroline, not the twins, nothing but this wonderful, exciting day. When they pulled up by the steep path that led down to the forestry road Mory was grinning from ear to ear. Dancer jogged to go on.

"No, girl," she said and followed on behind Lionel. She had filled him in on the disastrous party and he

had shrugged.

"What do you expect if she's there? She's trouble. So is them twins." He had looked aggrieved when she told him about the water fight. "Wish I'd been there."

Mory had laughed. "If you had been we'd never have been allowed to go today."

"They're about," he said. "Her and them twins. We passed them on the way up the lane to Llangabby."

"We'll keep a lookout," said Mory. But she didn't care. Nothing was going to spoil the day. It was going to be the best yet. She was determined.

When they arrived at the secret alleyway, the five of them cast cautious glances about before going into the den. All was as they had left it and they set about making the ponies comfortable. Felix went into the tunnel and found the rope and dragged out some firewood. He helped Lionel rig up the tether and then jumped and pulled at the branch to snap the wood into smaller pieces. Mory had forgotten the axe.

"Rabbit," said Lionel.

"No!" cried Mory.

"Too late." And there was Ben with a limp, grey, furry creature dangling from his mouth. But even a dead rabbit was not going to spoil Mory's day.

"Just don't let me see you skin it," she said. Putting her tack in the pile she undid her saddlebags. She pulled out her swimming costume and towel and went

into the tunnel to change. "I'm going swimming," she announced when she came out again.

"I'll come with you when I've watered the ponies," said Cara.

"Oh," said Mory, giving Dancer an apologetic pat. "I forgot about that."

"I don't mind doing it."

"You'd better use that bucket after all the trouble I had bringing it," said Felix. "I've got bruises."

"Thanks, both of you." Mory gave Felix's knee a quick inspection. "You'll live," she said and was gone.

Mory ran, letting gravity speed her down the slope between the trees. The running was effortless, like flying and the leaf mould soft under her bare feet. The sound of the waterfall guided her to the rock pool and, arriving at its edge, she dropped her towel and plunged straight in to burst to the surface, gasping and spluttering with the chill. She swam a little way until she had acclimatized to the icy temperature, then dived. Pulling herself with wide sweeping strokes she cruised the stony bottom. Then up to the ceiling of dazzling brightness which her arms shattered as she burst into the air. Turning on to her back she floated, staring up between the canopy of branches into the brilliance beyond.

She lay like this for several minutes until she had a sense of no longer being alone. She righted herself. Caroline and the twins stood round the edge of the pool, spaced at a neat distance to make a getaway difficult. Behind her the waterfall tumbled.

"Hell's bells," she muttered. "How did they find us?" Then she remembered. Hector! How could she have been so stupid? The same dog, at this place and the yard at Black Rock. Sunday night had been a giveaway in more ways than one. She had forgotten all about Hector giving them a fright. Her mind raced. Just because they had found the pool didn't mean they had found the rock alleyway. Almost certainly they hadn't. You had to know it was there. She dog-paddled.

"Hello, you guys," she said with as disarming a smile as she could manage, edging towards the shallows.

When her feet touched the bottom she stood up, shook droplets from her hands and put four fingers in her mouth. She blew. At first nothing happened. Her fingers were too wet. She tried again. A shrill blast sent a piercing warning through the woods, followed by another and another. The twins charged but too late. Mory splashed through the water and pushed Caroline out of the way. She grabbed her towel and ran.

"Get her, you idiot," shouted Phoebe. But it was too late. She could lead them on a goodly chase now far away from the secret den. She looked back. One of the twins was on her knees in the pool yelling at Caroline. She must have tripped. The noise of waterfall was too loud for Mory to hear what she was

saying. But Caroline was sitting on a rock in what looked like a huff. Mory slowed. Well, if they weren't going to follow it was all right with her. She would make her way back to the den.

She ran on up the slope crossing between the trees this way and that, ever cautious. She trod with a little more care now for her feet had warmed up and were sore. Thank goodness she hadn't worn her jodhpur boots to the pool. She might have lost them. One of her toes was bleeding. She wrapped the towel around herself and lifted her foot to get a better look.

Suddenly, she was rolling over and over. Someone sat on top of her and there was nothing she could do for her arms were pinned by the towel. She looked up.

"Felix!" She glared daggers. "Get off. This is serious. They're down by the rock pool. Didn't you hear my whistle?" With a grin, Felix unrolled her.

"Sure did," he said. "We all came running, except Cara. She's lookout again. Lucky we heard you before she went swimming too."

"I don't mind being ambushed by them, but I do mind being ambushed by you. Idiot." Mory shook the bits of twig and leaf from her towel. "Look we've got to get everyone back to the den and get holed up. They'll never find us in there. It's a lot easier to get jumped on in the woods."

"I just proved it," grinned Felix.

"OK, OK," said Mory. "Let's find the others before the enemy find them first." Ben came trotting between the trees, wagging his tail, with Lionel following.

"What's up?" he asked. Mory quickly explained.

"They must have come back because of Hector," she said.

"Course they would," said Lionel. "Why didn't we think?"

"Too late now," said Mory. "Let's get back before they come looking."

Ben suddenly stiffened and pointed with his nose through the trees. It was Josh moving stealthily towards them with his hand on Hector's collar. He beckoned them over and they followed him up the road. He showed them three mountain bikes buried under a pile of newly pulled bracken.

"Hector found them," said Josh. "They're well hidden. You can only see them up close."

"Leave them," said Mory. "They don't know where we are. Now that I've got away they may think we've all moved on."

"Got away," said Josh. "From who?"

"I got ambushed." She glared at Felix. "Twice! First time by them." Josh looked from Mory to Felix and back again.

"And second time?"

"Ask Felix. Come on, I'll explain when we get back. We don't want it to happen again."

Before they filed along the alleyway Josh doubled back to make sure they hadn't been followed.

"So far so good," said Mory and they hurried into

the den, leaving Lionel crouched at the entrance with Ben to make extra sure they hadn't been spotted.

Cara climbed down from the lookout and Josh turned the rabbit, which was slowly roasting on the wooden spit he and Lionel had made. Felix whittled a stick as a meat skewer and Mory rinsed her feet in order to inspect the damage before going into the tunnel to put on her clothes. When she came out again everyone was sitting round the fire watching the rabbit cook, including the dogs.

"Felix told us what happened," said Josh when she joined them. "You know what? I think we should do a little ambushing of our own."

"Maybe," said Mory. "But wouldn't it be better to let them get fed up with looking for us and while they do we could explore the cave." Felix's eyes lit up.

"Yes, I like that idea better." Lionel fidgeted and looked away.

"At least we can track them," said Josh.

"Two teams then," said Mory. "One for the cave and one for tracking." Lionel nodded. Felix spat on his palm and offered it. The others followed suit and shook, except for Cara. She didn't want to do either and once again offered to keep guard.

"But that's boring," said Mory.

"I like it," said Cara. "The view from up there is stunning and this time I brought a book."

"Each to his own," Mory said. "Food first?" Lionel nodded.

"This is cooked," he said.

"Rather you than me," said Mory and went to fetch some sandwiches. She was looking forward to exploring the cavern and wondered if they might find some bats. Along the tether line the four ponies stood dozing, their tails flicking the occasional fly. Suddenly starving, Mory held up a sandwich and took a huge bite.

ELEVEN

Cavers

After stuffing herself full Mory lay in a patch of sun with her eyes shut. It was Felix who jerked her out of her reverie with a gentle prod, eager to explore the cave. Cara was already on her way up to the lookout with a book between her teeth and Josh and Lionel were getting ready to be hunters.

"I'm not sure you should be going after them," said Mory. "It's so risky. Why don't you come with me and Felix?"

"No, ta," said Lionel. "Someone's got to be with the dogs. Can't take them in there."

"They'll wait." Lionel, uncomfortable at Mory's insistence, turned quickly to Josh.

"You coming?" Josh was torn. He wanted to go tracking and he wanted to explore the cave.

"It might be better to let Caroline and the twins go," he said. "Mory's right, we don't want to give this place away."

"I'll go on my own," said Lionel. "Give Ben a run." Josh was hesitant for a moment.

"No, it's OK," he said. "I'll come with you. Better if there's two."

"Just be careful," said Mory.

"Who are you telling?" said Lionel. "You be the same. There's tunnels under all these hills. Potholers go down. They have safety gear. So watch it."

"We will," said Mory, mindful of the warning. She certainly didn't want to get lost underground. The thought made her shiver. Lionel was right. They must take care. She got up and opened her saddlebags. She found the spare torch battery and stuffed it into her pocket then checked her torch was working properly.

"Any sign of the enemy?" Josh called up to Cara. Cara put down her book.

"Can't see anyone," she said. "Are you going after them?"

"To track them," said Josh.

"Don't give us away."

"Don't worry, we won't," said Lionel. "We're seeing what they're up to."

Mory was taking potholing safety seriously. She was knotting together several pieces of baler twine.

"What's that for?" asked Felix, impatient to go.

"So we don't get lost."

"Maybe it's a labyrinth?" said Felix. "Like Theseus and the Minotaur." Mory looked blank. "Theseus, the famous Greek warrior! He had to go into this labyrinth and kill the monster Minotaur. We did it at school. He had a magic ball of thread."

"What are you on about?" asked Mory. "The twine might be useful, that's all." She wound it into a skein and knotted it. "See you, Cara."

"Don't get lost."

"Don't you start. We're only going to look round the cavern bit." Felix grabbed Mory's tee-shirt and pulled.

"I'll be Theseus. You can be the Minotaur."

"Roar, roar," said Mory, giving him a shove.

Once in the tunnel it took a moment or two for their eyes to accustom themselves to the dark. Mory stared into the black. It was surprisingly cold after the sunshine and she shivered, feeling goose-pimples on her arms.

"Shine the torch this way," said Felix.

"Stop bossing me," she hissed, shining the thread of light over the rough tunnel walls. The distant sound of water drew them along the bumpy floor towards the cavern. "It's a bit spooky."

"It's not," said Felix. "It's great. A road to the centre of the earth." Felix's attitude was reassuring and she let the light lead them on. She shone it upwards and only then realized they were in the cavern. It was vast. Felix broke the silence.

"It's like a great building," he said. "Rock going up and up."

"A dungeon, more like," Mory replied. She shone the light across the craggy roof which was broken by fissures and cracks making secret and impenetrable chimneys.

"We could have a fire in here. The smoke would just go up."

"Be cave people," said Felix. "We might find dinosaur bones and things."

"Fossils?"

"Axe heads made of flint."

"Maybe," said Mory. "And maybe not." She kept her voice low and let the torch beam explore as far as it could in this surprisingly huge underground space. "Without the torch we could really get lost. From where we are we can't see daylight any more." Felix looked round. It was true. They had come further into the cave than before and the tunnel entrance was far enough away for the daylight to be obscured.

"I don't care what you say," Mory declared. "It's spooky." The running water had an eerie echo and she wanted to go back into the sun. She was almost shivering.

"Shine the torch over there again," said Felix.

"Where?"

"Back the other way. Look, it's another tunnel. I bet it is."

"Hang on, Felix, I don't think we should go too far. We could easily get lost. This place is pretty confusing."

"We've got the string."

The twine was looped over Mory's arm. She wasn't sure she wanted to go further in. She was wondering why potholers potholed. It was pretty unappealing, she thought.

"We can tie the end to this bit of rock and unwind it. Just like Theseus," said Felix.

"Hell's bells, Felix, what for?"

"So we know when we get back to here which direction the way out is." Mory sighed and shone the torch, letting Felix untie the twine. He knotted an end round the rock and began unwinding it. Mory lit the way, wishing she'd never thought of twine.

"Be careful," she said, grabbing him. "Don't go backwards into the dark like that. Let me shine the torch first."

"Fusspot."

"Fusspot nothing." The sound of the water was

getting louder and the tunnel began to go downhill, gradually at first but then more and more steeply. The twine ran out.

"We'd better go back," said Mory.

"Why?" said Felix. "We can't get lost in a tunnel. The only way back is that way. The string is there to guide us across the cavern to the outside." Mory let out another sigh. She was not enjoying this at all. She hated the way the darkness closed in, muffling sensation. If they lost the torch they would be in real trouble. They went a couple of steps further and Mory grabbed Felix. The tunnel fell away from them, funnelling steeply down into the dark. Felix was shaken. If he had gone one more step he would have fallen. The only way down was backwards like going down a ladder and it didn't look as if there were many footholds.

"That's steep!" Felix said, above the noise of the water. "There's an underground river down there somewhere. It might be the waterfall."

"It probably is," said Mory, realizing that the direction the tunnel was taking might well lead to the top of the fall. "But forget it. We're not going down there to find out."

She led the way back up and was relieved when they found the end of the baler twine. They were following its guiding line back into the cavern when a sudden, sharp and piercing cry penetrated the dark. It echoed round and round and became a hundred cries swirling around the cavern. Mory felt a stab of fear.

"Hell's bells," she whispered. "What's that?" The torch beam caught Felix full in the face. He looked terrified. She grabbed his arm and they stumbled across the cavern until they saw daylight at the tunnel entrance. Then they raced, gasping, spluttering and burst into sunlight. The brightness hurt. They shaded their eyes and stood panting, trying to rid themselves of the panic.

They had more or less recovered when Josh, Lionel and the dogs ran from the alleyway. At the same moment Cara slithered to the ground from the look-out. Even the ponies woke up.

"There might have been an accident," shouted Josh.

"Phoebe climbed the waterfall," added Lionel in gasps. "Said she couldn't get down. Then disappeared."

"Caroline and the other twin were calling for her. That's when we asked what the matter was."

Mory remembered the dreadful cry.

"I think we may have heard her. There was a terrible yell."

"Like the Minotaur," said Felix. "Dead scary."

"It echoed up the tunnel we were in. We think it leads to the top of the waterfall. We'd better go and see if we can find her."

"Go back. In there?" said Felix. "No way."

"We've got to go for help," said Josh.

"We can't just leave her," said Mory. "We've got

rope. We can tether the ponies to trees in the woods. We've got light. Only two of us need to go for help."

"I'll go," said Cara, reaching for Misty's tack.

"You go with her, Josh," said Mory.

"Can't Felix?"

"Ponies and bikes don't go at the same speed," said Mory. "It's better if two go. Felix, you come with me and Lionel you go back down to the pool."

Felix looked horrified. "No way. I'm not going back in there."

"I'll come with you," said Lionel, pale under his freckles. "Thing is, if there's a chance of finding her we should. The girl might be hurt."

"Thanks, Lionel." Mory's brain raced. "Felix, you go to the pool and tell Caroline and Trish that someone has gone for help and that Lionel and I are going to try and find Phoebe. But don't tell them how and keep them down there. Remember the den is a secret."

"Sleeping Cloud keep all secret. Sleeping Cloud fly," yelled Felix, running down the alleyway with Hector at his heels.

Lionel slipped a piece of baler twine through Ben's collar.

"We'll keep Ben with us," he said. "Never know, he might be useful." He tied him to the sapling. By the time Cara and Josh were tacked up and mounted, Dancer and Ning were tethered to trees away from the den.

"Take care," said Cara, and then she and Josh were gone, trotting between the trees to the forestry road.

There was no time to waste. Mory pulled on her sweatshirt, remembering how cold it had been underground, and slung the coiled tether rope over her shoulder. Lionel untied Ben and Mory led the way into the cave, shining the torch along what was beginning to feel a familiar route. Lionel and Ben kept close behind.

"I know exactly where we're going and it's quite safe," she said to reassure Lionel. She thought him incredibly brave now she knew how much he hated being underground. She had seen the trapped look in his eye as the darkness had closed around them.

"Take care, that's all," said Lionel, half panting. "Don't want anything happening to you."

They were in the cavern now and Mory searched the ground until she found the twine snaking into the dark.

"You bin this far?"

"Yes," said Mory, feeling Ben brush against her leg. The dog was pulling to go forward. "It's another tunnel. Felix was keen to explore it. Then he nearly fell down this steep funnel thing. After that we heard the yell and came out fast."

"Find her then, Ben," said Lionel. "Search her out. What can you smell, boy? Go on. Follow the scent."

"Don't go too fast," said Mory. "The string runs out before the drop." They reached the end of the twine and Mory shone the torch ahead. The beam picked out where the floor fell away. At the edge of the steep funnel Ben raised his nose.

"Anyone down there, boy?" said Lionel. "What can you smell?" Ben barked. Once, then twice.

"Hello," called Mory. Ben barked again. There was nothing but the sound of running water. "Phoebe! Hello! Phoebe!" There was a rattle of loose rock. "Phoebe is that you?"

A sound like a sob filtered up to them followed by a voice tense with fear.

"I can't see anything."

"Just stay where you are. We've got a torch. Are you hurt?"

"My arm is. I fell." Mory shone the torch as far over as she could into the depths below. More rocks clattered and way down a pale face came into view. "Oh, thank goodness. I can see your light."

"Stay where you are, Phoebe. Don't move," Mory called, then to Lionel she said, "I'm going down."

"You can't," said Lionel.

"I can tie the rope around my waist and we can anchor it."

"What on?"

Mory shone the torch. There was nothing. "Dancer."

"Dancer!" exclaimed Lionel. "Don't be soft."

"Do you think we could get her in here?" Mory could see he was weighing up the chances.

"Blindfolded we might," he said.

"We've got your old blanket to take the strain of the rope around her neck. You can hold her. I'll only use the rope if I have to. But if her arm is hurt Dancer might have to pull Phoebe up."

"That's fine if we can get Dancer in here."

"We've got to try." Mory leant over the drop again. "Phoebe, can you hear me? It's going to go dark again but we'll be back in a few minutes. Then I'll come down. OK?"

"OK. Please, don't be long."

"Just stay where you are. We'll be as quick as we can."

Ben led the way back to the outside. The first thing Mory did was to change the torch battery.

"We can't afford for the old one to die on us when we're in the middle of things," she said. Then she found matches and the half candle. "These might be useful." She shoved them in her pocket and fetched the old blanket and her towel.

"Better put a bridle on," said Lionel. "I'll have more control in case she does try and bunk off."

It was not many minutes before Dancer stood bridled with the rope wrapped in the blanket knotted around her shoulders. She showed no kind of alarm, not even when Mory gently wrapped the towel over her ears and eyes and tied it underneath with twine.

"Come on, girl," said Mory, leading her forward. "We're going to do some rescuing. Shine the torch, Lionel." Lionel took a deep breath.

"Ben, stay," he said and led the way into the tunnel. Mory followed with Dancer, blinded and trusting, going where she was led.

"Come on girl, good girl," said Mory. "Good girl."

Lionel shone the light and slowly they made their way along the tunnel and across the cavern. Dancer stumbled and blew through her nose. But she seemed relaxed, unafraid, not even minding the trip.

"Steady girl, steady," said Mory, in her most soothing tones. "You're a wonderful pony. A wonderful girl."

"She's never going to turn in that tunnel," said Lionel. "You're going to have to back her in." Lionel lit up the floor and Mory turned Dancer ready. At first the pony was confused but the gentle pressure Mory put on her shoulder aided by Lionel on the other side got her going backwards one step at a time down the slope.

"We must stop when we reach the end of the twine," panted Mory.

"That's now," said Lionel. Mory reached into her pocket for some pony nuts. As soon as Dancer smelt them her lips scooped them up and she crunched.

"I knew she was going to surprise you," said Mory. "She's the sort of pony that always does."

"So far so good," said Lionel, paying out the rope. He took the reins and waited while Mory pulled out the candle and matches.

"Shine the torch," she said. "Stop." There was a small ledge big enough to rest the candle on. She set it down and fumbled for a match. She struck it and held the flame under the candle until it had melted a pool of wax on to the ledge. When the candle was sitting firm in the cooled wax she lit it. The flame flickered but not enough to go out. She realized now, when they needed it, it wasn't much more than a stump.

"I'll have to take the torch," she said.

"I know," said Lionel. "You tell me what to do. I shan't see what you're doing when I'm holding Dancer."

"We'll take everything nice and slowly," said Mory.

"Good luck," said Lionel, his face tense in the flickering light.

"And to you." Mory gave his arm a quick squeeze before shining the torch down below.

"Hello, Phoebe," she called. "I'm going to drop a rope and then I'm climbing down to get you."

TWELVE

Brought to Light

Going down the side of the funnel was not easy. Mory took the strain on her arms and felt for footholds. It was impossible to see properly for the only way to keep the light on was to clamp the torch between her teeth. Now she knew why miners had lamps in their helmets; both hands were needed underground. Her main fear was that she would slip and land on top of the already injured Phoebe. The lower she went the louder the sound of the water, her only comfort the rope which brushed her face from time to time and was there if she wanted it. But the rope was a last resort. A sudden pull might frighten Dancer. The rope was for Phoebe.

Then it happened. A small miscalculation and her foot slipped. She clung on, fingers like hooks, against the rock. She gasped with the effort, opening her mouth enough for the torch to escape. It clattered down the slope leaving her blinded. Looking up, she saw the pale flicker of the candle. That was all that was left before total darkness. She froze, forcing

herself to breathe to calm the thud, thudding of her heart. Slowly, feeling for each foothold, she went on down.

The light, when it came on, was such a surprise she thought she imagined it. It shone up from only a metre or so away.

"I've got the torch," said Phoebe. "It landed by my foot." Level ground being so close Mory let herself slide to meet it. She squatted by Phoebe for a moment thinking how incredibly lucky the torch only got switched off and not broken when it fell. Then she stood up.

"Lionel," she called. "Can you hear me?"

"Yes." Lionel's voice came clear through the tumbling water.

"I'm down safely. I'll give you a shout when we're ready to go."

"Don't be long. The candle's flickering terrible."

"Dancer OK?"

"Fine."

Phoebe handed Mory the torch.

"I had trouble switching it on with one hand," she said. "I'm so cold."

"Thank goodness it landed where it did," said Mory. She mustn't lose the torch going up. It would be disaster. "Is it just your arm that's hurt?"

"I can't move my hand," said Phoebe. "I slipped. I must have put my arm out. When I tried to get out this way I didn't think about the dark. You see, after I climbed up the waterfall, I couldn't get down again. Stupid really, only it was a dare." She paused. "Thanks for finding me. It's really nice of you after ... well, everything."

"Phoebe," said Mory. "Listen." She put a hand on the girl's shoulder to find her shivering with cold and shock. "Cara and Josh have gone for help. We can stay here and wait or we can try and get you out. At the top of this slope which is not so very far up, look." And Mory shone the torch up to show her. "Up there is the way out. Lionel's there with Dancer. Now see this rope?" Phoebe turned up her tear stained face. "I can tie this round your middle, give Lionel a shout and you can let Dancer pull you up. Do you want to try it?"

"I want to get out."

"The thing is, if we wait, it could be for hours," said Mory. "And you're already freezing."

"I don't want to wait."

"Can I have a look at your arm?" Phoebe had the damaged limb clasped to her side.

"If I don't move it, it doesn't hurt too much."

"Right," said Mory. "I'm going to switch the torch off for a second. OK? It'll save the battery." That done she put the torch in her pocket and pulled off her sweatshirt. She shook it out and switched the torch on again. She found a place in the rock to wedge it so the beam shone at a convenient angle. "Can you stand up?" She put her hand under Phoebe's good arm and helped her to her feet. "I'm going to make a sling."

As gently as she could, Mory tucked her sweatshirt under the elbow of the hurt arm. Then she pulled the sleeves up and round Phoebe's neck and tied them. Pulling a piece of twine from her pocket she gathered the loose end of the sweatshirt and tied it, taking the twine up to fasten off around the sleeves. When she was satisfied nothing was going to come undone she took hold of the torch to give the improvised sling a final inspection.

"How does it feel?"

"Easier," said Phoebe. "Where did you learn that?"

Mory grinned. "Been watching the First Aid programmes on the telly. First time I tried it. Cool, eh?" She took hold of the rope.

"Lionel," she called. "Stand by. I'm going to tie the rope round Phoebe now. Dancer still OK?"

"Go ahead," came the reply.

Mory hoped the rope would be strong enough. After all it was brand new. And she hoped Dancer wouldn't panic when she felt the pressure. She sent calming thoughts to her pony and tied the rope around Phoebe's waist.

"Ready?"

"I think so," said Phoebe.

"Lionel, she's coming up. Don't rush."

"I'll go steady," called back Lionel. "Don't forget I'll be going into the dark. I can't take the candle. I

need both hands for Dancer." Hell's bells, thought Mory. I hadn't thought of that. She was going to stay at the bottom and light the way for Phoebe. In the end it was easier than Mory could have imagined. When Dancer walked forward Phoebe leant back against the rope and abseiled up the slope. The rope must have been tight but Phoebe was up in moments. As she reached the lip of the funnel and disappeared over Mory cried, "Stop!"

She shoved the torch between her teeth. Climbing up was a million times easier than climbing down. It wasn't long before she too was heaving herself over the funnel's lip. The candle was still alight but only just. Any minute and it would be out. Phoebe stood hunched, trying to undo the rope.

"Did it hurt much?" Mory asked.

"Not too bad. I couldn't have done it any other way."

"You were brilliant," said Mory. "I couldn't believe it as you went up. It was fantastic. So were Dancer and Lionel." She shone the torch down the tunnel. "Everything all right, Lionel?" she called.

"Fine," he said. "Be as quick as you can. Dancer's getting restless."

Phoebe held the torch with her good hand while Mory struggled with the knot. Above the noise of the water she could hear Dancer snorting. At last the knot came undone.

"Steady Dancer," Mory called. "Steady girl."

Phoebe shone the light ahead and they walked slowly up the tunnel, Mory coiling the rope as they went. Behind them the candle gave a last flicker and died.

"You OK?" Mory asked. Phoebe managed a "yes" through her chattering teeth. "We'll be out soon. It's not far now." Mory moved gently round Dancer and took the bridle from Lionel. Somehow he'd managed to undo the rope around her neck.

"Lionel, you were brilliant," Mory said. "Can you take the torch from Phoebe and get the blanket round her? She's freezing." Mory caught a glimpse of Lionel's pale face in the torch light, then turned her attention to her pony. "Steady girl, steady." She fished in her pocket for some pony nuts which were just what Dancer needed to stop her fidgeting. The pony munched contentedly. They had done it. They only had to get themselves out from underground and everyone would be safe. Mory put her hand on Dancer's neck.

"Not long now," she said. "You're a good pony." Unexpectedly, Dancer shook her head and the towel slipped down her face and fell to the ground. Mory expected an explosion but Dancer blew through her nostrils and shook her head again as if to say thank goodness that's off.

"Dancer OK?" Lionel asked.

"Fine," said Mory. "But the blindfold's come off." She reached for the towel and put it round her neck.

"Phoebe and me better lead the way," he said.

Lionel wrapped Phoebe in the blanket and put his arm around her shoulder to guide her along the tunnel and across the cavern.

"We're following the baler twine," he told her, his tones comforting, like when he talked to a pony. "Be outside any second." Mory followed, keeping Dancer at a safe distance.

Once across the cavern Mory saw Phoebe and

Lionel's stooped silhouettes against the daylight and at the tunnel entrance another black shape, Ben with his tail wagging. Dancer lunged forwards and Mory hung on.

"Steady," she said. "The light's going to be bright when we get outside. Just steady."

The light was bright, sharp, welcoming and warm. As the four of them acclimatized to the fresh air and space, Mory gently raised the blanket over Phoebe's head.

"This is our secret place," she said softly. "We're going to lead you from it so it can stay secret. Hope you don't mind." Phoebe didn't object. She was so relieved to be out of her dark prison she trusted them to lead her anywhere. Mory led Dancer down the alleyway. From the trees came the long whinny of a deserted and lonely pony. Dancer whinnied in reply. When Ning saw them she swung round on her halter rope. Lionel lifted the blanket from Phoebe's head and went to Ning to give her a reassuring pat.

From further down the hillside came shouting. The voices set Lionel running back along the alleyway to collect their remaining tack. He returned with it before Phoebe had noticed he'd gone and just before Trish raced between the trees to her sister.

There were tears and talk and recriminations. When Caroline caught up she let rip in her usual tactless way.

"Where have you been? Going underground was

the most stupid thing you could have done," she said. "Trish and I nearly died of worry."

"I don't expect Phoebe feels too good about it either," said Mory. "It looks like she's broken her arm."

"And you can shut up for a start, Mory Harper."

"No, you shut up, Caroline," said Trish. "Give it a rest for once." Caroline was stung into silence. Mory moved away and tacked up Dancer.

"Not much changes, does it?" said Felix, giving her a grin. "You got her out all right then? Was she the Minotaur?"

"I suppose she was," replied Mory. "She must have screamed when she fell."

It wasn't long before both ponies were tacked up and ready to go.

"Phoebe," said Mory. "Would you like to ride Dancer? We should get you home as fast as we can."

"I don't think I could get on," said Phoebe, looking white and drawn.

"There's a rock over here you could use as a mounting block," said Felix helpfully.

"Want to try?" Trish asked, full of concern for her sister. Phoebe gave a nod. The rock was a perfect height and Mory and Lionel helped her on. Phoebe held the front of the saddle with her good hand and Mory led Dancer slowly forward.

"What about Phoebe's bike?" asked Caroline. "I suppose you expect me to push two of them."

"We can take it in turns," said Felix. "It won't be

that bad."

They reached the forestry road and began the long walk home. Phoebe slumped on Dancer's back and the pony, as if knowing she had to go with care, plodded like a seaside donkey.

"You're a good girl, Dancer," whispered Mory, running her hand along Dancer's sleek neck.

"I think so too," said Phoebe and gave Mory a waxen smile. Mory smiled back.

They had reached the forestry gate when the Land Rover bumped towards them round the side of the hill and drew up sharply. Uncle Glyn jumped out and Cara, Josh and Aunt Olwen followed.

"We've got her," cried Mory as they drew near.

"It's Phoebe. I think she's broken her arm."

Aunt Olwen lifted back the blanket which was still around Phoebe's shoulders. She noted the sling.

"It's her left arm, Glyn. Better lift her down from the near side?" It took but a moment for Uncle Glyn's strong arms to gather Phoebe from the saddle.

"It's all right, Phoebe," said Aunt Olwen. "We'll soon have you feeling more comfortable." Uncle Glyn carried Phoebe to the Land Rover and lifted her gently inside.

"What about her bike?" asked Caroline. It was her turn to push it.

"I'll ride it back," said Josh, only too pleased.

"Can I come in the Land Rover with you?" pleaded Trish.

"Yes, of course," said Aunt Olwen.

"Looks like you've got a bike too, Cara," said Josh. Cara picked up the bike from where Trish had dropped it.

"You're all to come straight home," said Aunt Olwen. "And Lionel, you'd better turn Ning out with the others. She'll have to go back to Penyworlod tomorrow." With that Aunt Olwen climbed into the Land Rover and Uncle Glyn drove off. Mory swung herself into the saddle and Felix sped off, leaving Josh and Cara hurrying to catch up.

"If you think I'm rushing up that path like those three maniacs then you've another think coming," said Caroline. "Anyway, I want to know how you got

Phoebe out. That boy Felix said you'd lower her down the waterfall. That's why we waited. So how did you get her out?"

Mory let out a silent groan and caught Lionel's eye. He rubbed his nose with the back of his hand and said nothing.

"You'll have to ask Phoebe if you want to know," replied Mory. "You'll only say you don't believe us if we tell you." The den was a secret and she was going to keep it that way. She wasn't telling Caroline a thing. She and Lionel turned their ponies for home. Somehow, some awful how, they'd got stuck with Caroline Spencer again.

THIRTEEN

Showjumpers

"Well," said David when they were sitting at the kitchen table eating a late supper. "It was Mory to the rescue!"

"Me and Lionel and Dancer," corrected Mory.

"And me and Cara to get help," said Josh. "Someone had to do that."

"What can the girl have been thinking of to climb up the waterfall?" wondered Sheila.

"Maybe it was a dare," Mory said, remembering what Phoebe had told her.

"You'd have thought she'd have more sense. I hope neither of you would do anything so silly." Fortunately they didn't have to reply because David broke in and pointed out the obvious.

"She won't be able to do it again for a while. Not with a broken arm."

"And no more mountain biking till it mends," said Josh.

"Anyway," said Mory, thinking it best to change the subject. "We've got the Llantrist show to think about.

Lionel's entered Ning for the novice showjumping. Do you think I'll be able to beat him?"

"You've got to beat me and Rustler first," said Josh. "Anyway, why isn't Lionel in the intermediate with Cara?"

"Because Ning's too inexperienced for the bigger jumps, that's why," said Mory.

They'd just started pudding when the telephone rang. Sheila answered it and talked for ages. They were clearing up by the time she put down the receiver.

"That, as you probably guessed, was Mrs Spencer. Phoebe is fine you'll be glad to hear, although she did break her arm. They haven't been back long from the hospital."

"Is it in plaster?" Josh asked.

"I expect so. Now, Mrs Spencer sends special thanks to both of you and is asking everyone who helped in Phoebe's rescue to a special barbecue on Sunday."

"Oh, no!" said Mory. "Well, I'm only going if Lionel's invited."

"Of course he's invited. He was an important part of the rescue team."

Mory slumped down at the table and put her face in her hands.

"I'll never rescue anyone ever again. Things only get worse if you do."

"Oh, Mory, it won't be that bad," smiled David.

"Want to bet? Phoebe'll probably be all right and

maybe the other twin. But Caroline never ever is. Well, I shan't think about it until after the show."

When Megan and Lionel came over the next morning to collect Ning, Mory told Lionel about the barbecue. He looked at her astonished.

"I'm to go too?" he asked. "Me?"

" 'Fraid so," said Mory. "I'm not going if you don't. Anyway, I'm not thinking about it. What I am thinking about is how to beat you at the Llantrist show."

"You could easy," he said and grinned. "But I shall try hard not to let you."

"That's what Josh said," said Mory, grinning back.

The rest of the week was busy. Mory worked hard practising for the show and in the moments when she wasn't riding, cleaning tack or pulling Dancer's mane, she worked at her sketch plan. She was going to draw it on the wall only when she was certain she could no longer improve it. But already the Dancer in the plan looked good. Then David gave her a final pile of pots to box up.

"I'm taking them to London next week," he said.

"Next week!" said Mory. "Which day?"

"Looks like it'll be Tuesday!"

Mory was overjoyed.

"Can I ring Hannah and tell her?" she begged. She had been longing for Hannah to stay. Hannah, her best friend from Waring School when they had lived in Surrey. They had played table tennis together every day. They had been a real team. At last there was a definite date when David would collect and bring Hannah to Wales. Mory could hardly wait.

"I hope she likes it here. I hope she likes Dancer. She will Dad, won't she?"

"I can't imagine a single reason why she shouldn't," smiled David. "Not one."

Saturday came at last and all the preparations for the Llantrist Show began to seem worth it, especially when Mory stood in the line for the Best Turned Out Pony and was called forward. She came fourth, beaten, not surprisingly, by Cara and an immaculate Misty who came second and two others she didn't know. It was a good start to the day.

"I knew it was a waste of time me entering," said Josh, who didn't come anywhere. "I can't be bothered

with all that plaiting and stuff."

"But you'll make up for it in the Handy Pony," said Cara. "You and Rustler are so quick."

There were some very fast ponies in the Handy Pony class and Mory wondered if Josh would win after all. She watched him go round. He was determined and Rustler loved it, he fairly whizzed between the bending poles. After seeing his fast time Mory was sure he would win. The class was a disaster for her. She and Dancer managed to open and close the gate and jump the line of yellow and blue barrels. That was as far as they got. Dancer point blank refused to walk between the corridor of car tyres hung with bunting. In desperation Mory dismounted and led the pony through, then she rode her back between the tyres to prove a point.

"The bunting doesn't bite," she told Dancer. But it made no difference to the result. They were eliminated. Mory pinned her hopes on the showjumping.

At last she spotted Lionel and gave him a wave. He came trotting over on Ning.

"You didn't do the Handy Pony," said Mory.

"Not worth it on Ning."

"It wasn't worth it on Dancer. We got eliminated."

"Not bad for a pony who goes down tunnels and pulls people out of pits," laughed Lionel.

"She didn't like the bunting or maybe it was the tyres."

"That's ponies," said Lionel, shrugging.

"Is Caroline here?"

"Not coming," said Lionel. "Megan said." Mory brightened at the thought of no Caroline Spencer.

"Have you put your name down on the board for the jumping order yet?"

"Not yet," said Lionel and they rode over together. Lionel held the ponies while Mory found the chalk.

"Josh is a keen one," said Lionel. "He's down to go fifth."

"I think Cara must have put him down," said Mory. "What's your number?"

"Twenty-one."

"Happy to go eleventh?" she asked.

"OK by me." Mory chalked up twenty-one in eleventh place. Then Lionel noticed the number on Mory's back. "Hey, you got thirteen."

"I'm trying to think of it as lucky," Mory grinned, chalking up her thirteen next to number twelve. "But it hasn't been so far. At least I don't have to jump thirteenth."

"Just enjoy it," said Lionel. "It's only a bit of fun."

"It's everything," said Mory. "But if Dancer and I get a clear round, I'll be pleased."

"Me too," said Lionel. "Though that doesn't mean I won't try and win."

Mory laughed. "You and Josh both."

"You mean, you're not trying?"

"I might," said Mory, knowing that more than anything she wanted to win but now the jumping was almost upon her could hardly dare admit it. It was obvious who the winner would be – Lionel. He was the best rider.

When the time came to walk the course Aunt Olwen and Cara held the ponies. Mory, Josh and Lionel went round together. It seemed straightforward. Mory recognized the big red wall and the easy to knock over zig zag planks.

"Borrowed from Penyworlod," said Lionel. "All the jumps are."

"Should be a doddle," said Josh.

"Should be," said Lionel. Mory said nothing. Already she could feel that little worm of nerves wriggle in her tummy.

"It's a nice course," said Lionel. "A figure of eight, see. Start along the side of the arena, turn across the centre, back round the other side, then back across the centre and there you have it. Eight nice jumps."

"Easy peasy," said Josh.

"Two strides between the double. You've done that loads of times in lessons."

"If you say so," said Mory. "I'm nervous already."

"Megan's golden rule," said Lionel. "Relax. Tension ruins everything."

"OK, OK. I'm relaxed, oh, so relaxed, I'll fall off my pony."

"No point in going that far," said Josh.

Mory's nerves grew worse not better. Josh didn't seem to suffer from nerves. When it was his turn, she watched him jump a brave if haphazard clear round. Mory didn't watch anyone else jump and rode into the collecting ring to prepare Dancer. After warming up for a while they knocked down the practice jump twice. Mory knew she was to blame, the pony was really edgy. It's just a bit of fun, she told herself. It's just a bit of fun.

"Keep calm," said Lionel, when he trotted past her for his turn in the ring. Four clear rounds and Lionel to go. Mory managed a smile but didn't watch him jump. She knew it would be a faultless round and she was right.

"Lionel Jones on Evening Serenade goes clear," said the announcer.

But now it was her turn. On her way into the ring she passed Lionel on his way out.

"Good luck," he said, nodding.

"Thanks."

Mory was soon cantering in a circle waiting for the bell to ring. She concentrated hard on the route she was to follow and, without realizing it, her nerves dissolved and Dancer settled at last. The bell rang and they cantered through the start. They were over the first jump, the rustic poles, before Mory even noticed and heading for the staircase, jump number two. Dancer pricked her ears and did not hesitate. She turned towards the third, a line of barrels and Dancer faltered. Mory put her legs on hard and the pony responded. She had to steady her for the gate

which came quickly and Dancer wouldn't listen. They got over it more by luck than judgement and Mory found herself on the wrong leading leg. She slowed to a trot. It was the wall next. They had to come at it right. She asked for a canter and Dancer settled to a steady rhythm. Mory looked for her stride, saw it and pushed the pony forward. Dancer responded with a flying leap.

"Steady, girl, steady," said Mory, eyeing the double which was coming up fast. "It's not a race." They took the first part and bumpity bump they were in the air for the second. Mory was together enough this time to lean into the bend and they set off on the correct leading leg turning for jump seven, a pyramid of yellow and white poles. There was a little hesitation but Dancer jumped them and the last fence, the zig zag planks were upon them. Mory didn't give Dancer a chance to hesitate again and they flew over them. It was a clear round.

Mory trotted out of the arena patting her pony, with a smile as wide as her face. She found the mints in her jacket pocket and fed Dancer three. Cara came and thumped her on the back.

"Brilliant," she said. "You've all gone clear."

Mory rode Dancer around the show ground waiting for the jump off. She felt the wriggle of nerves in her stomach again. This time she mustn't let it affect Dancer. And she had a decision to make. Was she going to race against the clock or just go for another safe clear round? She couldn't decide what to do for the best.

When the course was ready for the jump off Mory rode back to the collecting ring to check the route. The rustic poles and the barrels had gone. Mory gulped. The remaining fences looked a lot higher. Well, she knew Dancer could jump them so it was up to her.

There were five of them in the jump off. The girl who was going round now on a roan, then Josh, another she didn't know, then Lionel. She was the last to go. That was an advantage. At least she'd know what she had to beat. The roan went well until he came to the wall where he took off too early and kicked out a brick. Mory turned away. She wasn't going to watch Josh. It was too nerve racking. After his round, when he came cantering back into the collecting ring, she knew, by his face, he hadn't achieved what he'd hoped for.

"That was four faults for Josh Harper on Rustler. And the next to jump is number six, Karen Blatchet on Mouse." Hell's bells, Josh looks really disappointed, she thought. She had a sudden stab of nerves watching Lionel go over the practice fence and decided to keep busy while the next rider jumped.

"Come on, Dancer," she said. She walked, trotted and cantered the pony bringing her round at last to the practice fence. Dancer popped over it.

"That was eight faults for Karen Blatchet on Mouse. The next to go is Lionel Jones on Mrs Reece's Evening Serenade," said the announcer.

"Come on, Dancer, let's watch how it should be done," she said.

Lionel looked beautifully collected as he cantered to the start. Ning flew jump after jump in a controlled and, what looked to Mory incredibly fast, clear round. When Ning came out she was puffing and blowing but still full of bounce. Lionel stroked her neck. He was really pleased with her. Megan was by the entrance smiling.

"Lionel Jones and Evening Serenade go clear in twenty-nine point eight seconds."

Not much chance of beating that, thought Mory, trotting past Lionel into the arena.

"And the next to jump is number thirteen, Mory Harper on Midnight Dancer," said the announcer.

It wasn't until she was cantering around the arena waiting for the bell that Mory knew what to do. Why not? she thought. Why not? Beat him or bust. This was it then. The bell rang and she was off. The first jump was the staircase. Mory came at it almost too fast and Dancer stood off and had to put in a huge leap to clear it. That made Mory steady her up a bit. Turning for the gate, she saw the stride and was off. Dancer sailed over it. The pony had a rhythm now. It felt unstoppable. They turned, on the correct leading leg this time, for the wall.

"Steady, girl, steady." But Dancer was loving it. She put in a terrific leap and the double was upon them almost before Mory was ready. But here it

seemed Dancer took over. Jump, stride, stride, jump.
Wonderful! Mory cantered for the white and yellow
pyramid. Before she was over the pyramid her mind
had rushed ahead to steadying Dancer for the zig zag
planks. It was a surprise when the pony tapped the
top white and yellow pole. Never look back, flashed
the thought. The planks are coming. Mory said go
and felt a surge of energy run through Dancer. They
soared over the planks and galloped for the finish. It
was then that Mory looked back at the pyramid. To
her relief the top pole was still there.

"Brilliant, Dancer, brilliant," she cried, laughing
and stroking and feeling inside like she had achieved
something momentous. She had asked the pony for

everything and Dancer had given it. What a big heart she had.

"That was a clear round for Mory Harper on Midnight Dancer in a time of twenty-eight point four seconds."

She let out a gasp. She had done it. She had beaten Lionel. She could hardly believe it. Cara came running across the grass towards her and suddenly Lionel was at her side on Ning, a big grin on his face. He leaned over and gave her a friendly nudge.

"See, you did it. Told you you could." Mory grinned back, slid to the ground and flung her arms around Dancer's neck.

"Well ridden," Cara cried. "Stunning! What a pity Caroline wasn't here to see that!"

"The winners of the novice showjumping are first number thirteen, Mory Harper on Midnight Dancer. Second number twenty-one, Lionel Jones on Evening Serenade. Third number seventeen, Teresa Stevens on Mr Pim. Fourth, number nineteen, Josh Harper on Rustler and fifth number six, Karen Blatchet on Mouse."

"Dancer, you are the most wonderful pony in the whole world," she said.

"Mory, come on," said Cara. "You got to collect your rosette." Dancer nuzzled Mory's pocket in the hopes of a peppermint.

"In the whole wide world," repeated Mory, producing five as a reward.

Epilogue

Mory stared at the outline she had drawn on the white wall of David's pottery. The drawing had been admired by Mrs Ashfield which made Mory feel more confident. The paint brush waited, glistening with black paint. Mory took a deep breath and scythed the whiteness with a brush line along Dancer's back. She had begun and here was her pony being immortalized on the wall at last. The thrill of winning the novice showjumping was still with her as were the congratulations she received from the twins at the lunch-time barbecue. When Caroline realized Mory had beaten Lionel she appeared too stunned to say anything. And because Lionel had been there, standing by her side, part of the team that had rescued her cousin, there was nothing rude she could say without appearing petty and mean. For once even Caroline seemed to realize that. Mrs Spencer had showered them with thanks and Phoebe, during a private moment, had apologized for messing up her Dancer sketch. She said they shouldn't have done it.

EPILOGUE

Mory still wasn't sure she trusted the twins but for the moment she didn't have to worry. They were going to Corfu on Tuesday and taking Caroline with them. It was wonderful. It meant getting rid of Caroline and having Hannah to stay on the same day.

Mory ran the paint brush down Dancer's neck and filled the outline with care. She sighed contentedly. The summer holidays were getting better and better. There was so much to look forward to and best of all the One Day Event. Oh, hurry up Tuesday, when she could tell Hannah all about it.

HIPPO ANIMAL

Midnight Dancer
Elizabeth Lindsay

Ride into adventure with Mory and her pony,
Midnight Dancer

Book 1: Midnight Dancer
Mory is thrilled when she finds the perfect pony. But will
she be allowed to keep her?

Book 2: Midnight Dancer: To Catch a Thief
There's a thief with his eye on Mory's mother's sapphire
necklace – and it's down to Mory and Midnight Dancer
to save the day…

Book 3: Midnight Dancer: Running Free
Mory and Dancer have a competition to win. But they
also have a mystery to solve…

Book 4: Midnight Dancer: Fireraisers
There's trouble on Uncle Glyn's farm – because there's a
camper who loves playing with fire. Can Mory and
Dancer avert disaster?

Look out for:

Book 5: Midnight Dancer: Joyriders
Book 6: Midnight Dancer: Ride By Night

HIPPO ANIMAL

*If you like animals, then you'll love
Hippo Animal Stories!*

Thunderfoot
Deborah van der Beek
When Mel finds the enormous, neglected horse
Thunderfoot, she doesn't know it will change her
life for ever...

Vanilla Fudge
Deborah van der Beek
When Lizzie and Hannah fall in love with the same
dog, neither of them will give up without a fight...

A Foxcub Named Freedom
Brenda Jobling
An injured vixen nudges her young son away from her.
She can sense danger and cares nothing for herself –
only for her son's freedom...

Pirate the Seal

Brenda Jobling

Ryan's always been lonely – but then he meets Pirate and at last he has a real friend...

Animal Rescue

Bette Paul

Can Tessa help save the badgers of Delves Wood from destruction?

Take Six Puppies

Bette Paul

Anna knows she shouldn't get attached to the six new puppies at the Millington Farm Dog Sanctuary, but surely it can't hurt to get just a *little* bit fond of them...